Laurence Brooke

The Queen of Two Worlds

Vol. 1

Laurence Brooke

The Queen of Two Worlds
Vol. 1

ISBN/EAN: 9783337324964

Printed in Europe, USA, Canada, Australia, Japan

Cover: Foto ©Andreas Hilbeck / pixelio.de

More available books at **www.hansebooks.com**

THE QUEEN
OF TWO WORLDS

BY

LAURENCE BROOKE.

IN THREE VOLUMES.

VOL. I.

𝕷𝖔𝖓𝖉𝖔𝖓:
SAMUEL TINSLEY & CO.,
10, SOUTHAMPTON STREET, STRAND.
1879.

CONTENTS.

CHAPTER IX.

PART I.

The World of Bohemia.

The Queen of Two Worlds.

CHAPTER I.

MARRIED IN HASTE.

LOCOMBE, a town situated on the Yorkshire coast, was one of those recently-developed watering-places which owe their existence to the favour of fashionable doctors and the facility of railway communication. In an incredibly short space of time it had emerged from insignificance into a wide expanse of picturesque villas, handsome shops, commodious lodging-houses, and first-rate hotels. But as it has no connection with this story, save in the matter of the one incident without

which the story itself would have had no
existence, the time of the reader will not
be wasted in the perusal of further and
unnecessary description.

One of the handsomest shops in the High
Street was that belonging to Mr. Joshua
Tubbs, the chief draper of the town ; and, on
a certain spring morning, Mr. Tubbs walked
to the door, and surveyed the scene before
him with a pleasant and benignant smile.

There were several reasons for this more
than ordinary cheerfulness. In the first
place, he was a leading citizen, a shining
light among the righteous, a man whose
voice uplifted at vestry or on platform commanded the attention of the thoughtful. In
the second place, his business was flourishing
enough to enable him to look forward with a
serene spirit to the morrow. And, in the
third and last place, his handsome and
favourite daughter Martha was going to
marry a gentleman of old family and fair
fortune, named Gabriel Vanstone. It may
be as well to take the opportunity of stating
that Gabriel Vanstone and Martha Tubbs
are *not* the hero and heroine of this story.

The affair had happened thus. Gabriel Vanstone, a young man, possessing more money than wit, had found his constitution so impaired by late hours and the consumption of a great deal too much champagne, that his doctor had advised him to betake himself to the pure and bracing air of Slocombe, until such time as he should be restored to his former self. The young fellow, used to the genial life of clubs and country-houses, found the place insufferably dull, and, after a few days' trial, had made up his mind to quit, when an incident occurred which scattered his resolution to the wind, and made him regard Slocombe from a totally different point of view.

Finding himself in need of a pair of gloves, he walked into the first shop he came to, which happened to be Mr. Tubbs', and was served by a young girl, whose first glance made his heart beat as it had never beaten in his life hitherto, and whose second made him fall head over ears in love with her.

This handsome young lady was no other than Miss Martha Tubbs, whose presence behind the counter on this particular day was due to the sudden illness of the principal shopwoman ; for the fair Martha had a horror of business, and had secretly resolved within her own soul that if she could not marry a gentleman she would go to her grave in 'single blessedness.'

Next day the foolish young man went in for some more things that he had no need of, but the purchase of which enabled him to gaze at the fair creature who had so enthralled him. Her dark sparkling eyes, her clear blooming cheeks, her pearly teeth, which had made so powerful an impression upon him the first time, effected his conquest the second. He was too much in love to think of consequences ; was his own master, with a clear fifty thousand pounds invested in good securities, and snapped his fingers at the probable disgust of his relatives. Waylaying Miss Tubbs as she was walking in the fields one evening by herself, he poured out his raptures in her greedy ear, and offered her his hand and future.

Miss Tubbs blushed, and after a little maidenly hesitation, let him see that his society was rather pleasing to her than otherwise. She even allowed him to press a kiss upon her chaste and blooming cheek, and then informed him that he must speak to papa. Mr. Vanstone intimated his more than willingness to seek an interview with Tubbs *père* upon the subject, for though weak, he was not vicious, and his intentions were strictly honourable.

After a little hesitation, Mr. Tubbs gave his consent. In his own private judgment, he considered the young man a fool, and he had also some old-fashioned notions as to the desirability of young women marrying in their own sphere of life. But Mr. Vanstone's folly was no concern of his, and it was for Martha a brilliant chance, which would never come more than once in a life.

The lovers were engaged, and were to be married at the parish church in a fortnight from the morning on which Mr. Tubbs walked to his shop door, and looked forth with that pleasant expression to which we have referred. As he stood there, his glance fell upon a young man who was crossing the road to him. He recognised the porter of the 'Christopher,' one of the best hotels of the town, and greeted him with a condescending nod.

'Good morning, Jinks! Did you want to speak to me?'

'A letter for you, sir, from a gentleman who arrived by the 11.30 London train last night,' replied the man named Jinks.

Mr. Tubbs looked at the strange handwriting, and wondered who on earth the gentleman from London could be. He opened the letter, thinking this would be the readiest method of plucking the heart out of the mystery, but when he had read it he was more puzzled than ever.

'Sir,' wrote his mysterious correspondent, 'I should be glad if you would call upon me as soon as you can conveniently do so, as I have something of importance to communicate to you, which it will be to your interest to hear without delay. You will oblige me by keeping both this letter and your visit a secret from everybody, for reasons that will be explained by yours faithfully,— GEORGE TREW.'

The worthy draper had never been so

surprised in his life. Who in the name of wonder was Mr. George Trew, and what could be the nature of this communication which necessitated so much mystery? Mr. Tubbs put on his hat, and entering the 'Christopher,' which was not five minutes' walk from his own shop, requested to be shown into the room occupied by his unknown correspondent. Mr. Trew rose at his entrance, and bowed courteously; he was a little gentleman—neat almost to primness in his dress, with a sharp eye, and a decided manner. Said the draper to himself, 'This man has got the cut of a lawyer, or I'm very much mistaken.'

He was not mistaken, for the little man told him his business in the first words he uttered.

'Good morning, Mr. Tubbs; you have been very prompt indeed. Can I offer you a glass of sherry—no—well it *is* a little early. I suppose you were very much surprised by the receipt of my letter. My presence here is soon explained. I am solicitor to Mr. Michael Vanstone, and it has come to his ears that his nephew is on the point of contracting a marriage with your daughter.'

Mr. Tubbs turned scarlet and stammered out, 'Your information is quite correct, sir.' He had an uneasy suspicion that in spite of Mr. Trew's suave address, he must appear in the lawyer's eyes a designing fellow.

'You will permit me to point out to you some of the disadvantages which will result from this match—disadvantages, I mean, which concern the young lady,' continued the little gentleman, throwing one leg over the other, and settling himself back in his chair, with the air of a man who is about to enter into an exhaustive statement.

Mr. Tubbs sat bolt upright, preserving strict silence. His experience of the world had taught him that in discussions of this kind the advantage rests with the man who hears all his opponent has got to say before he opens his own lips. Mr. Trew, whose policy on the present occasion was one of perfect frankness, proceeded with his reasons.

'Your daughter, like all ambitious young ladies, doubtless considers this a fine opportunity of advancing her own interests and getting into a sphere superior to her own. Now I can tell you that in this hope she will be grievously disappointed. I speak plainly, but I perceive that you are too much the man of the world to be offended with my plainness—men of Mr. Vanstone's class have a horror of trade. I think I may safely predict that not one lady among her husband's acquaintance will ever invite her to enter her drawing-room.'

The natural pride which all men feel in their offspring was a little roused at the uncompromising frankness of the lawyer's speech.

'Allow me to inform you, sir,' interrupted Mr. Tubbs in his most dignified way, 'that my daughter, in spite of her connection with trade, is not without education or accomplishments. She has been taught the piano by Mr. Thumps, the first music-master in Slocombe, and she can chatter French as fluently as you can English, which is saying something, for you seem a pretty glib one.'

'I am very grateful for your compliment,

and I have no doubt that Miss Tubbs is a most agreeable and accomplished young lady,' replied the little man with an affable smile; 'but even the fact of having enjoyed the tuition of Mr. Thumps, and of being able to speak French fluently, will not procure her admission into society.'

'I always understood, sir, that when a man married, he raised his wife to his own level, no matter what her previous position,' cried Mr. Tubbs hotly. 'I can give you instances in this country, for the matter of that, among the aristocracy of England itself.'

The lawyer shook his head with a calm persistence that was very provoking to a man who had long been accustomed to shake his own head at the crude ideas and rash utterances of others.

'You can quote examples to support every theory, Mr. Tubbs, but there are cases and cases. Lord A. or B., who owns half the county, may succeed in forcing people to be civil to his wife, but a plain gentleman like Gabriel Vanstone does not lead society; he is led by it. And society, Mr. Tubbs, will shut its doors in your daughter's face.'

For the first time since the unregenerate days of his youth, Mr. Tubbs made use of a wicked expression. 'Then all I have to say, sir, is, that society may go to the devil.'

'It will go there, Mr. Tubbs, at its appointed time, not before. Come, sir, I think we are getting a little too warm over the matter. I have taken this journey at the request of Mr. Michael Vanstone in order to try and arrange the business in a friendly spirit.'

'Mr. Gabriel is over age, his own master, and I don't see what right his relatives have to interfere,' said the draper, doggedly. 'When I married, I didn't ask the consent of my uncles and cousins.'

'Well, well, sir, we will not argue that particular point, but pass on to another, and one of vital importance to the young lady. I think I have succeeded in proving to you that she will not accomplish the principal object for which she marries, namely, securing an entrance into good society. Now let us see how her failure will affect her domestic happiness. Without any particular disrespect to Mr. Gabriel Vanstone, he is an amiable, but a rather weak young man.

'Just a little soft, perhaps,' assented Mr. Tubbs, in a more gracious tone.

'Quite so. Now, it is well known that fickleness and weakness generally go together, and when young Vanstone finds that his marriage has made him lose the esteem of his friends and relatives, it is almost certain that he will vent his chagrin upon the woman whom he considers to have been the cause of it all. You can see yourself, Mr. Tubbs, what a pleasant prospect will be hers then—nominally the mistress of a good home, with the title of a gentleman's wife, and wealth enough to give her every possible comfort—but shut out from society, despised and neglected by her husband. This is not a fate that she would embrace willingly, but it is the fate that she will embrace, if she takes advantage of his calf-love to bind herself to him for life.

The lawyer ceased, pleased to observe that his impressive words and tones had considerably shaken Mr. Tubbs' obstinacy. The draper sat silent, pondering these things in his heart, and then Mr. George Trew leaned forward and played his trump card.

' Now, sir, you are a man of business ; I am the same ; and I hope we shall be able to understand each other without difficulty. To relinquish this match will be a painful blow to yourself and daughter. My client has taken this fact into his consideration, and on his behalf I am empowered to offer you two thousand pounds to break it off, and to give your daughter a thousand when it is done.'

' It is not the filthy lucre that tempts me, sir,' replied Tubbs, with an incorruptible air that would have been perfect save for the wistful look which came into his eyes at mention of that pleasant sum ; ' but what you have just said touching my girl's future happiness, has made a very powerful and painful impression on me.'

' I'll be hanged if the impression would have been so powerful but for the bribe of the two thousand,' thought the lawyer to himself, then he said aloud : ' You will act much more wisely by breaking it off than letting it go on. The thousand pounds will make her a capital dowry against the time she meets with some nice young fellow in her own walk of life. It is very seldom, Mr. Tubbs, that good comes from marrying into a different station.'

'I must own that I have often thought so myself,' said the draper.

'Well, is it to be a bargain, Mr. Tubbs? I can draw up a little form of agreement between us in five minutes.'

'But there's Martha to be made to see all this. It wants a man with your gift of the gab to persuade her that a thousand down is better than two thousand a-year for life.'

'Come, come, Mr. Tubbs, you can manage that, I am sure : you have authority in your own house, I suppose?' replied the lawyer, smiling.

'But Martha is a difficult one to manage : she has a touch of her poor mother's temper, —Heaven rest her soul,' explained the father, who, great as he was in the world of Slocombe, had suffered himself to be somewhat easily led at home by his favourite daughter.

'Well, of course, if your authority fails. I will see what I can do with her. But she is evidently a young woman of sense, and would see these things clearly enough if they were once put in a proper light. You can send her away somewhere, taking good care that Gabriel Vanstone does not know where she is to be found.'

The lawyer dipped his pen into the ink and began to write out an agreement, while Mr. Tubbs looked on in a rather agitated frame of mind. His moral senses had got rather confused, and he could not determine quite satisfactorily whether he was doing the best for his daughter's interests, or whether he was basely selling the chance of her happiness and prosperity for the sum of two thousand pounds. 'That lawyer chap has so muddled my poor head with his jabber, that I can't think clearly,' he said to himself, as he listened to the rapid scratching of Mr. Trew's pen.

'Now then, Mr. Tubbs, just sign your name to this,' and he rapidly read over what he had written.

Then Mr. Tubbs rose up, buttoned his

coat and spoke in the slow accents of a man who has arrived at an important conclusion.

'Mr. Trew, I should like to well weigh this matter before I put my name to any contract. You must remember, sir, that I am a parent, and that I must lay my head upon my pillow this night with the full conviction that I have done my duty; that of the two alternatives which are offered to me, I have chosen that which will ensure her the most perfect chance of happiness in the future. I must have time, sir, to reason and examine; for, although I am not a rich man, and the two thousand would come in very sweet just now, it is not merely a matter of money with me. . I am a father, and the welfare of my children is dearer to me than all the gold in the world.'

As Mr. Tubbs uttered these sentiments, his homely features lighted up with feeling, a dignified pathos in his voice, even the lawyer, in spite of his mortification at any delay in assenting to his proposals, could not help feeling moved.

'As you please, sir, as you please.   When

do you think you can promise to give me an answer? My client, Mr. Michael Vanstone, is naturally anxious to hear the result of my mission.'

'I will call on you between six and seven this evening, Mr. Trew, and give you my final decision. I will now wish you good morning, sir.'

'Good morning, Mr. Tubbs, good morning. I shall expect you between six and seven.'

Mr. Tubbs, deep in thought, walked back to his shop. Entering the parlour, the first sight that greeted his eyes was his daughter Martha seated on the sofa by the side of her lover.

'Papa,' said Martha, advancing towards him, covered with blushes. 'Gabriel and I have been very very wicked. We have been married this morning privately.'

Mr. Tubbs fell back two or three paces in his astonishment, and Gabriel Vanstone got up from the sofa and said in tones that just shook a little from the novelty of his situation,—

'The fact is, I thought if we waited any

longer, it might get to the ears of my relatives, and they might interfere to prevent it. You see, we have saved all bother of that sort now. We are going from here by the 2.40 train.'

Half - an - hour afterwards, Mr. Tubbs wended his way to the 'Christopher,' and related what had happened. The lawyer smiled with the calmness of a man whose experience of human affairs prevents him from being astonished any longer by either the follies or the crimes of mankind, and said,—

'I am very sorry, both for your sake and the sake of the family I represent. Your daughter is a clever young lady, but I think she will, sooner or later, repent the step she has taken.'

CHAPTER II.

GETTING INTO SOCIETY.

MRS. VANSTONE left her native town of Slocombe with a hopeful heart and elated spirit. Her airy castles were being translated to solid ground. She had reached the goal of her youthful ambition—marriage with a man of wealth and family; for to this young *bourgeoise* an income of over three thousand a-year seemed to promise an inexhaustible supply of pleasures and luxuries. She 'dipt into the future,' and was enchanted with the vision that she saw—a house furnished after the newest mode, an equipage unsurpassed in elegance, herself robed in magnificent toilets, and ablaze with costly gems receiving aristocratic visitors in her drawing-room. Poor, ambitious Mrs. Vanstone! If, as she flung her arms round the necks of her sisters and father, she cried and smiled hysterically, let us be charitable in our cynicism. From the small parlour of a draper's shop to her present proud prospects was an elevation that might well have excited the steadiest nerves. We cannot all retain in our prosperous hours that evenly - balanced mind which is recommended by the philosophical Horace.

There were a few drawbacks certainly. When Martha Tubbs, musing in her solitary chamber over the future, had exclaimed with the small heroine of Mrs. Browning, ' I will have a lover,' she had drawn the portrait of a man very different from Gabriel Vanstone. He was, as a matter of course, to be handsome, intellectual, one to whom she could look up, by whom she could be guided. Her present husband had none of these necessary qualifications—he was weak, vacillating, easily led by a will a little stronger than his own. However useful this weakness might prove, considering it from a strictly matrimonial point of view, the fair Martha in her heart despised him for it. Like all women, she would snatch at power where she could; while, like the majority of women, she would sooner have been governed by a more powerful mind.

As all these thoughts and speculations were at present in a germ-like state, Gabriel Vanstone had nothing to complain of in his newly-made bride. Her great content with the present, her sanguine hopes of the future, —for Martha had that supreme confidence in her own ability to conquer hostile circumstances that has led many ambitious souls to successful achievement—gave to her manners a softness and tenderness that were charming enough to a young and desperately-enamoured husband. As Gabriel drove away with his beautiful prize, he thought that he was a man to be envied. In that moment of intense satisfaction, he would have said that the world could not be better lost than for love.

At any rate he was wise to bask in the sunshine of to-day, for the morrow might bring clouds, even upon the radiant counte-

nance of Martha.   Their marriage had been
accomplished easily enough, since it only required the consent of two people, one of
whom was desperately in love, the other
ambitious ; but the getting into society in-
volved the unanimous consent of persons
who were not likely to be influenced so
readily by Martha's beauty and accomplishments as her husband had been.   Her high
opinion of her own merits, and her ignorance
of a wider world than the small provincial one
in which she had gathered her experience of
life, made her feel sanguine as to the accom-
plishment of the task she had set to herself.
But Gabriel was pretty sure in his own mind
that she would be doomed to disappointment.

The season was far advanced, in fact
nearly ended, when they returned from their
wedding tour, and took a furnished house in
one of the small streets that abound about
Mayfair.   Having got a place to which they
could ask respectable people, the next thing
to do was to try and get respectable people
to come to it.   After much deliberation,
Gabriel resolved that he would go to his
uncle, and do his best to persuade him to

show a favourable countenance to his ple-
beian wife.

Mr. Michael Vanstone was a rich, old
gentleman of about sixty or thereabouts. He
was easily moved to anger, and unpleasantly
plain-spoken and uncomplimentary when in
that condition. It required, therefore, no
small amount of courage on Gabriel's part to
present himself before his offended relative.

'By Gad, sir,' was the old gentleman's
greeting to him, 'you must have the impu-
dence of the devil to look me in the face
after what you have done.'

'I am very sorry that it has offended you so
deeply, sir,' stammered his nephew, keeping
his eyes away from his uncle's wrathful glance.

'Offended me! offended me, sir!' repeated
Mr. Michael Vanstone with savage emphasis.
'I always knew you had a small share of wit,
but I would *not* have believed that you could
have made such a contemptible fool of yourself as to marry a linen-draper's daughter.
Good heavens! fancy a Vanstone marrying
a woman who had passed her life in selling
pennyworths of tape over a counter. What
an unmitigated blessing that my poor brother

did not live to witness this; it would have broken his heart, you foolish, you wicked, you criminal young scoundrel!'

It seemed that the irritated old man could not find epithets sufficiently vigorous to express his mingled contempt and disgust.

'Will you let me speak a moment, sir,' asked Gabriel, at length.

'Speak as long as you like!' roared his uncle, fiercely, flinging himself back in his easy chair, and muttering wrathfully to himself.

'What I wanted to tell you is this,' said the young husband, plucking up spirit, 'that although Martha—'

'What's her name?' called out the old man, with a shout that drove all the courage away from poor Gabriel's heart.

'Martha,' he repeated.

'Martha. Good heavens! what a name! I wonder it wasn't Mary Ann.'

'Well, sir, we will not quarrel over her name; that was given her by others. What I was about to tell you was this, that in spite of her want of family, my wife is neither common nor uneducated.

She has the accomplishments of a lady; she can play beautifully, she can speak French—'

'And paint on velvet, and accompany herself on the guitar; a complete *rara avis*, a kind of female admirable Crichton, I suppose,' interrupted Mr. Michael Vanstone, with an irritable sneer. Then he continued with savage energy, 'Who the deuce cares what she can do? All the world will want to know is—Who is she? and when that question is answered, it will very properly turn its back upon her.'

Gabriel was a good-tempered man, and was ready to make every allowance for his relative's prejudices; but he was also a husband, and this last insult made the cup of his patience overflow.

'Come, sir, be kind enough to remember that you are speaking of my wife. However contemptible she may seem to you, she is very dear to me. It is natural that you should feel offended at such a marriage, but the knot is tied, and there is no untying it. All I ask is that you will give her a fair trial, that you will let her prove to you that in spite of her origin she has the manners and feelings of a lady.'

'And now, sir, you shall hear my answer to this request,' said the old gentleman, grimly. 'You have made a fool of yourself, and you must take the consequences. I will not put forth my little finger to save you from them. You can come and see me when you like ; blood is thicker than water, and I don't want to be at daggers-drawn with my own brother's son ; but that wife of yours shall never enter this house, and I will never enter hers. You married Miss Martha Tubbs with your eyes open ; I wish you joy of your bargain.'

So resolute was the old man's manner, that Gabriel saw it was useless to supplicate his good offices any further.

'Then I suppose I must wish you good morning, sir.'

'Good morning,' replied the uncle, grimly ; then, as his nephew extended his hand, he added, in a softer tone, 'I tell you, Gabriel, that your idiotic conduct has pained me as I have not been pained for years. I would have given ten thousand to have got you out of the mess while it was possible. If you had not been so precipitate a fool, I am pretty sure I *should* have managed to get you out of it. You have ruined your future, and dishonoured your father's memory.'

Gabriel did not venture to contradict the old gentleman, but took his leave, and drove to the residence of his cousin Caroline, who had not long been married to Sir Francis Grahame, a rich baronet. He was in hopes that he might succeed better in this quarter, for he and his cousin had been brought up together as children, and had for each other a more than ordinary cousinly affection.

But Lady Grahame was as obstinate as his more plain-spoken uncle. She flatly refused to take up his wife.

'Had she been a poor gentlewoman, Gabriel, I would have done my best for her ; but to receive as my guest a girl who has stood behind a shop counter, *never !* Had I the will, I have not the power to accomplish what you wish ; did I give her the *entrée* here, she would never get friends. Her youth and her good looks are her greatest obstacles ; they will only attract the attention which is fatal. If you were both twice as old as you are, and had a daughter who could take the lead in your household, you might contrive to get her invited in return for your own dinners. But in the present condition of things, it is impossible. Society will never open its doors to your wife. If you try hard you may get around you a set ; but of what creatures will it be composed ? Of women of doubtful and un-defined position ; mere hangers-on of our world. Men you may get to visit you, par-ticularly as Mrs. Vanstone is handsome, but women never, except of the class I have just described.'

Gabriel looked perplexed. His cousin argued the matter so calmly, and yet with such iron logic, that he knew not how to refute her. He began to see very clearly that his ambitious Martha would never get a foothold in the unreachable world of good society.

'If your wife has married you on specula-tion, I fear she will be grievously disap-pointed,' added Lady Grahame, with a cold smile. Then she cried with a sudden impetuosity, 'Good heavens! Gabriel, were you mad when you took this foolish step?'

'I was very much in love,' replied her cousin, simply.

'Are you as much in love now, may I ask?'

'I think so,' replied the young man, with an awkward smile.

Lady Grahame tossed her head, and looked at him with a kind of contemptuous pity in her glance. 'I can predict that you will not be so much in love this time next year. I know enough of human nature to prophesy that your wife will be a rose so long as there seems a chance of gratifying her ambitious views; a thorn when she sees that chance melt away. Poor, weak, silly Gabriel, I didn't think your enemies could wish you a greater punishment than you will bring on yourself. As if I could not have found you a nice girl to-morrow if it was imperative that you should fall in love.'

Gabriel Vanstone rose. 'You might give her a trial, Caroline.'

Lady Grahame shook her head obstinately.

'No, my foolish cousin, one must draw the line somewhere—I draw it at the shop-counter. And I have already explained to you the uselessness of my inviting her here. Your future programme must be this :—you visit your relatives, and keep up your old club sets, while your wife is making belief that she is somebody among the shady circle she will get around her. I don't wish to be more offensive than I can help, Gabriel, but it is necessary to state plain facts plainly.'

'I will say good morning,' said her cousin, stiffly extending his hand.

'Good morning,' repeated Lady Grahame, mimicking his tone. 'Do not forget, Gabriel, that your family have a just right to feel offended by this marriage. A man is bound to fulfil his duties towards his family before he consults his own inclinations. I shall always be pleased to see *you* here, just as in the old days.'

So the young husband had to return home, and communicate his failures to expectant Martha. As might be expected, it proved a crushing blow to her; with their help an entrance into society would have been easy enough, she said to herself, but without their help the task seemed to grow into a difficult one. She shed some natural tears, for she felt that she was not being treated fairly; that these insolent people, who refused to open their doors to her, knew positively nothing of her merits and qualifications. For all they knew to the contrary, she might have the wit and genius of a De Staël : they rejected her simply on the narrow ground of being a linen-draper's daughter.

That she was a girl of courage and resolution was proved by the fact that, after the shedding of these few tears of wounded vanity and disappointment, the insolence of her husband's relatives awoke a spirit of defiance. They despised her—she would despise them.

'We will do without their invitations, Gabriel,' she cried, with flashing eyes. 'Since I cannot get into the society I want, I will make a society for myself. There must be some people who will be glad to eat our luncheons and dinners; they may not be of the best kind, but they will be better than nobody. As papa used to say,

"What are the odds so long as you are happy." '

This was a colloquial vulgarism for which, in her maiden days, Martha Tubbs had often rebuked her parent, but in her present turbulent and defiant mood she took rather a keen delight in casting off for a moment these shackles of gentility that might prove more galling than she expected.

So Mrs. Vanstone set dauntlessly to work to gather round her a little circle of friends and acquaintances, who would forgive her her lack of illustrious origin for the sake of her good dinners. This sort of thing is being attempted daily by hundreds of pleasure-loving matrons with about much the same results as attended her effort. Gabriel brought home some jovial card-playing young gentlemen from his various clubs, who generally contrived to win their host's money, and paid for a hospitality thus; they did not return otherwise than in the small coin of conversation and sedulous attention to their hostess. These pleasant-mannered fellows had a large acquaintance amongst a peculiar portion of female society—that portion which comprises women who live poorly and dress well, who can always pay for a bonnet, but find great difficulty in meeting the demands of the butcher ; women who never have any settled habitation, but flit about from capital to capital with their husbands and are at home everywhere, and are a kind of upper class Bohemians.

By one of these fair and worldly creatures was the young wife especially patronised, and as she was a sort of leader among her little world, she soon brought others. This lady was the wife of a Captain Polling, a poor officer, with whom she had run away from her father's parsonage. Bright, handsome, clever and vivacious, Mrs. Polling was glad to make the acquaintance of a woman who had plenty of money, could take her out in her carriage, and give her good dinners. To a critical judge, there was in this agreeable person's manners a strong dash of Bohemianism that might have been more repellant than attractive, but poor Mrs. Vanstone, ignorant of the great world, thought her a model of fashionable deportment, and copied her so far as she could. In many instances, the young housekeeper found her friend's experience and judgment of eminent use to her. When she gave her dinners, it was Mrs. Polling who superintended the arrangement of the *menu*, and instructed her in the various small details of etiquette which are so puzzling to the social novice. It was Mrs. Polling who accompanied her to the dressmaker and milliner, and advised her on the difficult matter of colour and style.

On the whole, Mrs. Vanstone was not unhappy. It is true she had sense enough to perceive that these people were mere hangers-on to the skirts of the society she had dreamed of entering; it is true that she could not yet boast of having entertained, or of having been entertained, by a lady of title. But still they were pleasant enough, they dressed well, they mingled enough at intervals with the world above them to catch something of its tone and flavour; they knew the latest fashionable intelligence, the last fashionable scandal: to whom Lord D— had proposed, whom the daughter of Lord E— had accepted. If she could not entertain the planets, she must be content with the satellites. It would have been pleasanter if her friends had possessed a little more wealth ; could have paid their visits in their own carriages, instead of in hired vehicles or on foot ; but you cannot have everything. One thing was very certain, this life was better than any that Slocombe could have offered her.

As for Gabriel Vanstone, he was also well contented. Awkward and shy, he did not care much for the society of fashionable women, and felt more at home among these well-bred Bohemians whose manners had neither coldness nor *hauteur*, and in spite of occasional displays of temper on Mrs. Vanstone's part, and a few unjustifiable acts of domestic tyranny, he was still devotedly attached to his wife, and far from repenting the step he had taken.

CHAPTER III.

A RASH BET.

AS they could not remain in London when their more fashionable neighbours had left it, and as none of their acquaintance had country houses to invite them to, Mr. and Mrs. Vanstone passed the autumn and winter on the Continent. And to her credit it must be stated that Martha did not forget the humble home at Slocombe : from Rome, Naples, Geneva, wherever, in fact, the newly-married couple pitched their tent, she despatched lengthy epistles to her father and sisters descriptive of the present place of abode, and detailing the various incidents of her new life. It is almost needless to say that these letters were a great event in the small

Slocombe circle, that their coming was eagerly expected, and their contents communicated to an admiring and awe-stricken band of friends and acquaintances, who had known the fair writer in the days of her youth before her sudden elevation to greatness.

They came back to London about the middle of March, having secured for the season the furnished house which they had occupied last year. Mrs. Vanstone was pleased to return to the metropolis, pleased to renew her festivities, her visits to the Opera and theatres, her drives in the Park, her elegant little dinners, her hundred-and-one pleasant occupations. Her husband shared her delight, since he had his own reasons for preferring London to the capitals of the Continent—he was fond of the society of his clubs, and when he was away from it, felt like a fish out of water.

A constant succession of small dinners (Mrs. Vanstone never entertained more than eight at a time) and other amusements soon made the time fly, and brought them within three weeks of the Derby.

'How I detest this race-time!' cried the vivacious Mrs. Polling as she sat in her friend's drawing-room after one of those dinners, in giving which Mrs. Vanstone took so keen a delight. 'There's a kind of Derby fever in the air—men can talk of nothing but odds, favourites, trials, gallops—a perfect jargon of the stable.'

Mrs. Vanstone smiled, but said nothing. In spite of her confidence in her own powers, her knowledge of her humble antecedents weighed upon her somewhat heavily in the presence of worldly creatures like the officer's dashing wife, and she allowed her guests to do most of the talking.

'I can put you up to a good thing, Mrs. Polling,' said a young man named Melton, who was standing near her.

'Just listen to the execrable slang; "put me up to a good thing,"' laughed the lady. 'Well, Mr. Melton, what is the good thing you are so kind as to wish to recommend me. Can I make my fortune?'

'That depends on how much you risk. The horse to back is Suzerain; you can now get fifty to one against him.'

' But is he certain to win ? ' asked Mrs. Polling, mockingly.

' Nobody can say that ; but I hear from good authority that—'

' I am much obliged to you for your advice, Mr. Melton,' interrupted the lively lady. ' But I am not rich enough to bet. The only event on which I ever do venture anything is the University boat-race : my wager then takes the form of gloves, and if I lose I don't pay.'

' What has Melton been recommending you for the Derby ? ' asked Captain Polling sauntering up to the two ladies.

' A creature rejoicing in the name of Suzerain, against whom we can get fifty to one,' replied his wife laughing.

' What in the name of wonder makes you imagine such a brute as that has got a chance, Melton ? '

' I have my information from very good authority,' said Mr. Melton, with an important air.

' Well, I never bet on races, but if I did, I should back Belisarius, Turnpike, or Warrior. Vanstone, have you made a book ? '

This question was addressed to the host, who was just passing them ; he stopped, and catching his wife's eye, looked a little confused.

' It's hardly worth calling a book ; I just back one or two for a nominal sum.'

But Mrs. Vanstone did not like that look of confusion, and when the guests were gone, she said to him in a serious tone, —' Gabriel, I do hope that you have never been addicted to betting and gambling, or that, if you have been, you will give them up at once.'

' My dear Martha, don't be so silly. Do you think I am such a fool as to risk more than I can lose without inconvenience.'

' You are not rich enough to afford to lose anything,' replied Martha, with some asperity. ' You lose at *écarté* in this house more than you ought, but I look upon that as a kind of tax one has to pay people for coming ; but there is no need to throw money away out of the house.' It will be seen from these pungent remarks that Mrs. Vanstone had plenty of that useful ingredient, common sense, in her composition, and rated the friendship of her guests at its proper value. She had also a holy horror of betting, the result of a certain episode in her own family history. Her uncle, Thomas Tubbs, a genial fellow, following the profession of a commercial traveller, had long ago brought his wife and children to the verge of starvation through too great a fondness for backing his fancy. Chiefly through the pious exhortations of his brother, he had been at length reclaimed, and now fled the race-course as he would a viper; but Martha had never forgotten the spectacle of that once wretched home.

She did not know that she had united herself to a man with the same fatal tendency. Gambling and betting were Gabriel Vanstone's two great and criminal weaknesses, and by them he had considerably impaired his fortune before he met his wife. He had not even confined himself to cards and racing, but had speculated also on the Stock Exchange. Ill-luck followed him everywhere; the horses he backed never won, and he universally got bad cards. When he bulled, some sudden and unforeseen Continental complication was sure to send his stocks down ; when he beared, some equally unforeseen complication sent them up. Every year did he resolve that he would never bet, speculate, or touch a card again, except for mere nominal amounts, and every year found him with a fresh deficit in his capital.

He unfortunately mixed with two sets of men—a poor set and a rich set. The poor set comprised fellows like Polling, who were gentlemen by birth and education, and contrived to live Heaven knows how ; the rich set contained men like Melton, who had inherited from their relatives large fortunes, or were able to raise plenty of present cash on the strength of their expectations.

Had none of his friends won more from him than Polling, he would have been able to stand the racket, but when removed from the watchful eye of his wife, Gabriel played with the rich set for high stakes, and generally lost. When he had returned to London this season, he had made a vow that he would never play again at cards for stakes beyond a certain moderate amount. This resolve he had managed to keep ; but on the other hand he had made a very foolish book on the Derby.

The night before the great festival, he conned over his bets with a grave face. There were several rash transactions, but the one that annoyed him most was one with his friend Melton. Discussing the merits of Suzerain one night, Melton had offered to take fifty to one in thousands, and in the heat of the moment Vanstone had laid it.

CHAPTER IV.

RUINED!

IT was evidently going to be a splendid day. The morning sun had risen slowly and majestically in a sky of faultless blue, and there was just enough breeze to comfortably temper the heat to those enthusiastic worshippers of our national sport who were going to take the road. Mr. Gabriel Vanstone glanced out of his dressing-room window with an air of satisfaction.

Of all festivals, the Derby stood first in his estimation, and the splendid weather gave the one thing necessary to complete enjoyment. Having finished his toilet, he went into the bedroom to take leave of his wife.

'Good-bye, my dear.' He stooped and kissed her affectionately.

'Good-bye, Gabriel,' said the wife pleasantly, then she added ; 'you are quite sure that you don't stand to lose much ? '

'Only a hundred or two at the worst,' replied Mr. Vanstone glibly, although his heart beat a little as he uttered the lie. Putting the bets against Suzerian out of the question, he had backed other horses to the extent of five thousand pounds, and unless one of these won, he would have to pay this sum on settling day. It was natural, therefore, that he should feel a little qualmish at his wife's question ; he felt that he had made a very foolish book this year, and inwardly resolved to be more careful when the next Derby came round.

'You must keep yourself very quiet,' he said as he left her. She was near her accouchment, and Gabriel Vanstone looked forward with great joy to the prospect of a son and heir.

A couple of hours afterwards the young husband was seated on the drag of his friend Captain Carter, bowling along that famous and dusty road, every inch of which has been described by countless pens.

' Have you heard anything about Suzerain ? ' asked Vanstone in the course of conversation —a conversation that, as a matter of course, ran upon nothing else than horses, and the doings of past Derbies.

' Who wants to hear anything about him ? ' replied Captain Carter, a good-looking young guardsman, who was ruining himself as fast as he could. ' He's a rank outsider ; you don't mean to say you have got anything on him ? I hope not, for your own sake.'

' But I have got something *against* him, laid when he was fifty to one, and the last odds were forty. I ought to hedge.'

' Hardly worth the trouble, I think,' replied Carter, carelessly. ' How much do you want to put on him ? '

' A thousand or more if I can ; for if I only put the same that has been given me, the difference in the odds would make ten thousand.'

' But, my dear fellow, Suzerain hasn't a chance, I tell you.'

' I don't say he has, but discretion is the

better part of valour,' replied Vanstone, who
was thinking of what his Martha would say
if she knew that he ran even the slightest
risk of losing fifteen thousand pounds.

'You must do it with the bookmakers;
Gregg is as good as anybody,' said the
captain, as they came in sight of the famous
Downs, crowded with its expectant thousands.

If not for the sake of the brief race, the
Derby is at least worth going to for the sake
of seeing the various types of humanity that
are congregated on that one spot of ground.
For some hours at least pleasure reigns
triumphant ; it shines on the face of the
noisy and somewhat too hilarious costermonger as he sits in that ricketty little cart,
which is to him what a drag is to a noble-
man—it finds its representatives in those
ubiquitous darkies, who sing their liveliest
airs, and play their loudest, in the full knowledge that on a festive occasion like the present coppers are bound to flow in abundantly
—it sparkles in the eyes of that youth who
has driven down with his sweetheart in a
hansom cab, and is as proud of his white

hat and green veil as a duke might be of a star and garter; honest delight, too, beams on the countenance of that same sweetheart, a pretty, smartly-dressed girl, with a tasty bonnet built by her own deft fingers, for she looks as if she were in the millinery line of business—for is she not seeing life in a mighty and pleasant fashion, and could she not fill three volumes with a description of all she sees on that teeming heath in the course of this too brief day. Even those blasé, over-dressed, deeply-rouged ladies who laugh very loudly, and perpetually quaff champagne, on the top of that drag yonder, seem to be gay for once with a gaiety that comes straight from the heart. A motley, incongruous group, met together for a few hours, and for a few hours united by the same sympathies. Ere night closes in, the vast heath will be as silent and deserted as a wilderness: the prince will have gone back to his palace, the noble to his mansion, the costermonger to his alley, the beggar to his den. The hopes and fears that have swayed by turns thousands of hearts during the last few weeks will have been ended by the rush of the winner past the judge's box. Thousands will have changed hands; while the winners bless and the losers curse the Derby of the year.

'What against Suzerain?' says Gabriel Vanstone to Gregg, the bookmaker, a burly, red - faced man, whom people remember twenty years ago as a billiard-marker at one of the West-end clubs. Mr. Gregg is supposed to be the richest man of his class now.

'Forty to one!' answers the Leviathan, with a smile. He knows Gabriel Vanstone well, and has done business with him before. In another moment the two men have settled their little transaction, and Gabriel goes back to the grand stand with a com- paratively light heart. It is true that if by any chance Suzerain should win, he will lose fifteen thousand pounds, that is, a quarter of his whole capital ; but what is that loss compared to the prospect of fifty thousand being swept away.

'Did you find Gregg friendly?' asks his friend Captain Carker, looking up from his note-book, in which he has been making some extensive calculations. It may be mentioned *en passant* that the gallant captain has never been known to win on any race yet.

'All right, I've hedged pretty well,' answers Gabriel, cheerfully. But as he speaks, conscience whispers to him that he has been acting very foolishly and culpably in staking his money on the speed of these four-legged creatures. He is not now a single man without ties, with nobody's future but his own to think about. In the words of a philosopher with whom he is but little acquainted, he has given hostages to fortune; and in imitating the reckless example of Carker and fools of the same class, he is squandering the patrimony of his child. He has staked on three horses, Belisarius, Turnpike, Warrior, and hedged on Suzerain. Reckoning up his chances, he finds that he stands thus,—if Belisarius wins, he makes seven thousand; if Turnpike wins, he loses two thousand; if Warrior wins, he makes a thousand; if Suzerain wins, he loses fifteen thousand; if none of these win, he loses five thousand. Two chances of winning against three of losing,—not an encouraging prospect. As he thinks over all this, he says to himself, 'I'm as big a fool as ever lived.' It is a pity that his uncle was not there to overhear this muttered remark, for the old gentleman would have endorsed it with the greatest heartiness.

'Awful bad luck I've had in my bets this year,' says Captain Carker, when he has finished his little sum. 'At the worst I lose twenty thousand; at the best I must lose two.'

'I'm rather better than that,' says Gabriel. 'I do stand two chances of winning, and the biggest loss is fifteen thousand.'

'I should be glad to exchange liabilities,' answers the captain, with a smile. He has inherited an immense fortune from his aunt, a rich ironmaster's widow, and will be able to go on losing like this for a few years yet ere he is finally ruined.

Hark, there goes the bell. The vast crowd is slowly being driven off the course, —men and women dodge under the railings and appear close on the other side, striving to gain a post of vantage from which they can seet he splendid rush of those magnificent creatures, on whose power, strength, and speed and endurance vast fortunes hang. It is an anxious moment—the lull before the storm. The wandering minstrel hushes his song, for he knows that everybody is too interested in the coming race to think of flinging him anything. Even the beggar drops his piteous whine, and glances at the glossy horses and the slender jockeys, with as much interest as if he had a thousand on the event.

Thousands of eyes are bent upon them as they take their preliminary canters past the anxious gaze of the spectators. Turnpike shows last, piloted by the crack jockey of the day, and Gabriel Vanstone turns a little pale as he hears the unanimous buzz of admiration which greets his appearance. Suzerain keeps in the background, as if conscious of his inferiority. They walk back again to the starting point, and slowly arrange themselves in line. Heads are craned round from every point to catch a glimpse of the first rush. The signal is given—there's a roar and then a sudden lull, that tells of a false start.   They arrange themselves again ·—another anxious moment, and then, to the cry 'They're off!' the whole field sweeps away, with Belisarius and Turnpike among the leaders.

The gaze of every man and woman on that heath is bent now upon the narrow strip of ground along which these swift animals dash like a whirlwind.   On they go, —their tiny jockeys crouching in the saddle, their firm and delicate hands guiding and restraining the ardour of their steeds, their keen eyes watching for the first opportunity of getting into a better place.   A third of the course has been traversed now, and the three favourites, Belisarius, Turnpike, and Warrior are nearly abreast, just a little behind some stable companions, who have made the running.   A few more seconds, and then it seems to all that the real race has begun.   Warrior is a noble horse, but he is evidently not equal to the other two. For some seconds, Belisarius and Turnpike draw near the goal, 'neck by neck, stride by stride.'   The air resounds with the shouts of

the respective backers of the two gallant
horses who are struggling so desperately for
the crown of victory. Then, inch by inch,
Turnpike begins to creep ahead of his exhausted rival. In vain does the defeated
jockey dig his spurs into Belisarius' flanks
till they are dyed in blood ; in vain does the
sharp, stinging stroke of the whip fall
heavily upon him. They are close to the
fatal corner, and it is pretty clear that Belisarius, good horse as he may be, is beaten.

So keen has the struggle been between
the two favourites, that the spectators have
hardly cast a glance at the field toiling in
their rear. But as they near that crucial
corner, a horse whose colours are unfamiliar
to most, creeps out of the compact mass, and
takes up his position on the left of Belisarius.
People turn on each other a questioning
gaze, that asks who is this new comer, and
then the air resounds with a hoarse murmur
of 'Suzerain,' forty to one against whom
has been laid freely at the post. To Gabriel
Vanstone those colours are known well
enough.

'Just my luck ; that brute will win,' he

says, with an oath, as the glass shakes in his trembling hand.

'Nonsense,' exclaims the contemptuous Carker. 'He may beat Belisarius, but he'll never get near Turnpike. Make your mind easy.'

For a few seconds there is a peculiar lull among the spectators, who see clearly enough that the advent of this rank outsider looks like mischief. Then, as the dark horse creeps past the exhausted Belisarius and draws up by the side of Turnpike, whose jockey is doing all he knows to save him from this unsuspected danger, the Babel bursts forth again, and the name of the new rival divides the air with that of the favourite.

There is not a hand's length between the two now, and the goal is terribly close. Turnpike's jockey makes one supreme effort, and succeeds in widening the distance for a second; but that effort is his last. The gallant favourite can do no more. The spurs are buried in Suzerain's flanks, the whip falls twice on his shoulder, and with the rush of an avalanche, the dark outsider sweeps past the judge's box, the winner of one of the most sensational Derbys on record.

'I may thank my stars I hedged,' says Gabriel Vanstone, as he turns away, pale and disgusted, from the spectacle which has cost him fifteen thousand pounds.

'Deuced quiet they've kept him,' remarked Captain Carker, who was as much suprised at the event as everybody else. 'It was Melton who took the bet, was it not? You may depend upon it that fellow was in the secret.'

'I'll never make or take another bet as long as I live,' cried Gabriel.

'My dear fellow, I make that resolution at the end of every Derby, but next year I've got as bad a book as ever,' said Carker, laughing.

Owing to the blocked state of the road, and the consumption of a pretty good amount of champagne at Carker's house, Gabriel Vanstone did not get back to his own home until nearly four o'clock in the morning. Great was his suprise to learn that his wife's accouchement had already begun, and that the doctor was in attendance.

He was more than slightly flustered by

the champagne, but this intelligence sobered him directly, and he enquired anxiously as to her state. The housekeeper, who had opened the door to him, shook her head gravely at this question, and said that the doctor should come and see him as soon as he could. In a few moments he came down to Gabriel, and informed him that Mrs. Vanstone was still in considerable danger.

The young husband was terribly moved. His wife was still little less dear to him than on the day when she had stolen quietly out of her father's house to marry him, and the thought of losing her in this way was unendurable. The doctor, a kind, grave man, did his best to soothe his fears, and gave him what hope he could.

The anxious hours sped on, and still there was no certain intelligence. Gabriel Vanstone paced up and down the library in his intense anxiety. In this new and terrible trouble, the loss of his fifteen thousand was forgotten.

The butler entered the room noiselessly, and put the morning paper on the table. When he had gone, Gabriel took it up with the listless air of a man who is hardly conscious of his actions, and glanced absently at the heading containing the principal items of news. Suddenly his eye lighted on a paragraph, whose terrible meaning flashed straight into his brain, bewildered as it was by this recent trouble.

'As we go to press, we learn that Mr. Gregg, the well-known bookmaker, committed suicide at a late hour last night, after his return from Epsom. It is said that he was driven to the rash act by his inability to meet the heavy losses he had sustained by the defeat of the favourite.'

The paper dropped from his hand, and he staggered wildly to the door, which was partially open, his face white as death, the beads of perspiration thick upon his forehead. And at that moment the wail of a new-born infant smote upon his ear.

'My God, my God!' he cried in his agony; 'my folly has made my wife and child beggars.'

And, under these conditions, under a roof on which ruin had thus suddenly descended, did Helen Vanstone, the heroine of this story, make her entrance into the world.

CHAPTER V.

THE VANSTONE HOUSEHOLD.

IN our last chapter, the Vanstone family were residing in the aristocratic neighbourhood of Mayfair. We must now skip a period of some eighteen years, and come to the moment when we find them located in a less distinguished quarter, Regent's Park.

There are many faded-looking and dingy streets in this part of the metropolis, and Thomas Street was about as dingy and faded-looking as any of them. The houses were of the usual forty and fifty pounds a-year type, that is to say, plain and unadorned to the point of repulsiveness. To this charming retreat had the Vanstones moved after their loss of fortune ; their income was

certainly miserably small, but it would not
have been difficult to choose a more cheerful
spot.   Mrs. Vanstone, however, who was
disposed to take even the smallest troubles
in a tragical spirit, had made up her mind,
after the first inspection, that the gentle
melancholy of Thomas Street was in harmony with their own sombre fortunes.   Mr.
Vanstone, who added meekness to foolish-
ness, offered no opposition to his wife's
mournful sense of propriety, and to Thomas
Street they moved.   Nobody who was not
well acquainted with Mrs. Vanstone's
character, could realise the grim satisfaction
that she took in glancing disdainfully down
the street which she had herself chosen, and
muttering wrathfully,—' Gracious Heaven !
to imagine that I should be forced to pass
my life in a hole like this !'

The surroundings were to her discontent
what the wind is to fire.   Did she feel it
slacken for a moment, she had only to go
to the windows of her small drawing-room,
and look opposite, to fan it into its pristine
strength.   Often and often of late years had
her husband mildly urged their removal into

a newer and more cheerful neighbourhood. Her invariable response had been—'What does it matter where we live now ? this place is favourable to the obscurity to which your criminal folly has condemned us.' To have taken her forcibly from Thomas Street, would have been to deprive her of her most cherished grievance : she was too cunning to deny herself so sweet a subject of complaint.

Yet if she was shrewish and disagreeable, some allowance must be made for her. She had early resolved to turn her beauty to good account, and this was the outcome of her resolution. Nothing exceeds the poignancy of having lost what we once enjoyed, of being driven ruthlessly from the Eden in which we passed so few yet such happy hours. The poor lady would have been more than an angel if she could have forgiven what she justly termed her husband's criminal folly, which had reduced her and her child to comparative poverty.

No stranger, happening to stray incidentally into the precincts of Thomas Street for the first time, would have been tempted to choose that direction again. Everything

about the place was so very dingy, wore
such an air of sadness, which one felt convinced must be in keeping with the fortunes
of their owners.   The doors were dirty ;
not fresh and bright with paint as in houses
where the tenants are never behind in their
rent, nor callous to the demands of the tax-
gatherer ; so were the blinds as a rule ; and
even about the muslin curtains, that made a
brave appearance in the summer, there was
an air of limpness characteristic of the neighbourhood.

And yet upon this gloomy soil there had
sprung up as fair a flower of womanhood
as ever the eye of man gazed upon, proving
that beauty can flourish with but an illiberal
supply of air, light, and sunshine.   When
Helen Vanstone came out of that dingy-
looking house, the effect was such as is pro-
duced on seeing a luxuriant tree growing in
some city oasis, and overshadowing with its
waving foliage the windows of dark rooms
in which men toil and labour.   The sunshine that flows for ever from girlish grace
and beauty flooded that sombre street as
she stepped lightly along it, conscious of her

charms, but half indifferent to, half despising the admiration which they attracted in such a place and from such admirers.

It will be seen from this trait alone that the girl was both proud and discontented, and not at all inclined to bestow her love upon a man belonging to the class among which her father's follies had placed her. Nor was this discontent unnatural. It had been implanted and fostered in her heart by her mother, who had done her best to teach her to look upon the father as an enemy whom it was impossible to forgive. Certainly Mrs. Vanstone had something to complain of in being reduced at one fell swoop from affluence to comparative poverty. It was true that she had married her husband not for love, but as a good speculation ; but what woman in her situation would ever remember this ? All she knew was that she had been prepared to make him a good and faithful wife, and that she had been shamefully ill-used. Even where married people love each other dearly, pecuniary misfortunes often bring shadows between them ; and in cases where there is no love,

unhappiness is sure to follow. Mrs Vanstone was possessed of a bad temper and a
bitter tongue. In the hour when her husband had faltered forth the history of their
ruin, she sought to control neither. She gave
utterance to words which she afterwards
owned to herself she regretted ; and for the
first time the foolish Gabriel suspected that
his wife had married him without a spark of
affection. He could have borne patiently,
and forgiven what would have been justifi-
able indignation, but he could *not* forgive
the insults which she heaped on him in the
mere wantonness of passion. He only
answered her once, and in those words he
buried all the love with which her beauty
had ever inspired him.

'I am much obliged to you for dropping
the veil with so little ceremony, Mrs. Vanstone. I am glad that I have at last learned
the state of your feelings when you stood
beside me at the altar. The majority of
persons would hold that you had been
rightly punished.'

His disgust and indignation at her coarse
avowals conquered for the moment his

habitual awe of her, and with all her contempt for him, she quailed beneath his glance
as he spoke thus.

From that hour there was no further
attempt at dissimulation on either side. As
the Gabriel Vanstone who could have given
her dresses and jewels, and maintained her
in luxury, she might have tolerated his love,
returned his caresses with a certain warmth
that came from gratitude. For the Gabriel
Vanstone whose criminal folly had brought
her and her child to this sordid existence,
her feeling was little short of decided aversion.

Where the income is limited, the man has
better chances of enjoying himself than the
woman. Needless to say that the affable
Polling and her satellites fled at the first
appearance of disaster, and left the woman
who had feasted them so often to weep alone.
In justice to Polling, it must be said, that
although intensely worldly, she was not
much of a hypocrite : she honestly owned
that she could not afford to waste her time
with poor people. From year's end to
year's end, therefore, poor Mrs. Vanstone

sat in that gloomy house in Thomas Street, the monotony of her life only relieved now and then by the visit of some companion in misfortune, with whose tears and lamentations over the past she could mingle her own. The husband, as it has been hinted, was better off. For a few guineas a-year he obtained admittance to a second-rate club, which contained some very pleasant fellows. In the company of these choice spirits he passed his evenings. Mrs. Vanstone affected to consider herself neglected, but in her secret heart was glad to get rid of him, and thought his absence cheaply purchased by so small a subscription.

There are very few women who do not possess the faculty of loving, and although Mrs. Vanstone had many qualities the reverse of amiable, she was not without it. Disappointed in her married life (and however we despise the motives that prompted her to accept her husband, we must own that it was a most crushing disappointment), she turned for consolation to her child. On the graceful little fairy, to whom every year seemed to bring a fresh beauty, a fresh charm, she expended all the love of her nature. Peevish and irritable to everybody else, to Helen she was always tender and gentle : when she addressed her, the eye and the voice involuntarily softened. Selfish in ordinary life, there was nothing she would not have deprived herself of to confer a moment's gratification on her child. Helen was the one bit of pure sunshine in her sombre existence.

And it was no wonder that the mother's heart so twined itself round her,—for although the girl had many faults, some inherent in her nature, some engendered by the conditions of her life, she was affectionate and loving. There was a certain impetuosity about her which betrayed an impulsive nature, and was a most charming trait. She was not strong - minded nor learned, nor particularly accomplished, but she had a big fund of that valuable quality, common-sense, which enabled her to see clearly through things that blind half the world. She had a profound contempt for convention, a bitter scorn of rich relatives, and a vocabulary that was furnished with a liberal supply of vigorous adjectives. 'I am a Bohemian,' she was accustomed to say of herself, with a charming smile, that made her look like a young Hebe.

But in spite of the hostile conditions of her life, the impress of gentlewoman was stamped upon her; refinement spoke in every tone, every gesture. If her phraseology was at times a little too blunt for the ears of fastidious frequenters of drawing-rooms, it proceeded from such beautiful lips, it was expressed in accents so musical, that you forgot to find fault,—you were ready to own that a phrase is not the same in one mouth as in another. She had grand dark eyes that looked at you frankly and fearlessly; dark brown hair clustering round a forehead smooth and white as marble; a mouth perfect in shape, and enhanced by brilliant teeth; a tall and slender figure.

Only once had this peerless girl mingled in the society she was fitted to adorn with her grace and beauty. This was at a ball given by her father's cousin, Lady Grahame, who had condescended to take occasional notice of them in their poverty; and seeing that Helen was as beautiful a girl as any that frequented her saloons, had been gracious enough to invite her. Need it be said that the day on which she received that invitation was one marked with white in her calendar? Delicious visions rose before her ardent and longing gaze. She would be able to mix among the great world for which she had so fervent an admiration: some handsome young hero of the Byronic and romantic type would lose his heart to her, and lay his fortune at her feet.

The inefficiency of her wardrobe was certainly a painful fact, for she possessed that exquisite sensitiveness which often anticipates misery, and felt sure that her poverty would be apparent to the eyes of all. But at seventeen, hope springs eternal in the human breast, and when the hour of setting out arrived, Helen forgot the meagreness of her attire, in expectation of the delicious novelties in store for her. How her young eyes sparkled and her young heart throbbed as she entered the rooms, and mingled in the crowd of richly-apparelled guests. She was not a shy or a timid girl ; but for the first few moments her father felt her hand tremble as it nestled on his arm. It was all so different from what she had been used to. She fancied that even the language of these aristocratic looking men and women must be different from that of her ordinary associates.

Lady Grahame spoke a few kind words to her, and found her a partner for the next dance. A woman of the world, and not bad-hearted, she was touched by the girl's beauty and embarrassment, and in her own mind secretly revolved schemes of advancing her fortunes. Helen's partner was a young gentleman fresh from Eton, rather shy and timid, but excessively polite ; and after she had become more used to the scene, her naturalness returned, and she collected her ideas sufficiently to carry on a very lively conversation. So agreeable indeed did she make herself, that the young Etonian went home and dreamed of her.

Alas ! her happiness was short-lived.

This dance over, she ensconced herself in an out-of-the-way corner, and presently overheard the following conversation between two exquisites who stood near her.

1st Exquisite.—'I hear there's a very pretty girl here, a poor relative of Lady Grahame's. Have you seen her?'

2d Exquisite, speaking in a tone of languid interest.—'No; but I shall make it my business to do so. I daresay a little attention will go a long way with her. Poor people are always grateful for very slight favours.'

The girl's blood seemed on fire, as she listened to these decidedly coarse remarks. She was not experienced enough to know that these brainless young men cultivated cynicism because they thought it made them appear men of the world, and would have spoken disparagingly of a Duchess. Her eyes filled with tears, an unpleasant lump rose in her throat, her lips quivered, and, rising swiftly from her seat, she walked into a little deserted ante-room, and burst into a flood of bitter tears. How she hated the ball, the people whom she had so admired,—her cousin and everybody connected with it ! Never again would she stir out of her own humble home to be the sport and jest of these insolent creatures.

'What is the matter ?' asked a voice close beside her. She lifted up her tear-stained face, and beheld Lady Grahame.

Unfortunately, Helen had inherited a good deal of her mother's temper. She was just at boiling point, now, in that frame of mind in which it is a relief to say bitter things, regardless of justice or consequences.

'I would rather not stay here any longer, if you please. I have been grossly insulted. You were very kind to invite me, I know, but I was foolish to accept. I am old enough to know that poor people cannot visit rich without loss of their self-respect.'

Lady Grahame drew herself up stiffly. Perhaps she had mistaken this young girl's character. She remembered that the blood of the Tubbs ran in her veins side by side with that of the Vanstones.

'I do not understand you, Helen; be kind enough to explain in what manner you have been insulted, and by whom.'

With flashing eyes and scarlet cheeks, the girl told her story. Lady Grahame's reply was dignified, yet not devoid of graciousness.

'I am very sorry that you should have overheard these rude young men, but your own good sense should tell you not to waste a thought upon what they said. You will oblige me by coming back into the ball-room, and I will find you a partner.'

It was unfortunate that this last part was spoken in a somewhat peremptory tone. To Helen it savoured both of dictation (another form of insult from the rich to the poor), and want of sympathy, and she hardened directly. It must also be borne in mind that her mother had inoculated her with her own cordial detestation of their wealthy relatives.

'I must beg that you will excuse me. I may be foolishly sensitive, but I could not enjoy myself after what I have heard. I would much rather leave at once.'

Lady Grahame hardened also at this un-conciliatory speech. It was not consistent with ber dignity to argue such a point any longer with a foolish and headstrong girl.

'As you please: if you stay here I will send your father to you.'

Mr. Vanstone came to her shortly, looking very embarrassed, for his cousin had been quietly cutting in her interview with him.

'My dear, you have offended Lady Grahame for life.'

'Papa, I don't care a straw if I never see Lady Grahame's face again,' replied Miss Helen emphatically. At that moment she spoke the truth; all the pride in her nature was aroused.

She went home, and poured her wrongs into her mother's ears. In her heart, Mrs. Vanstone regretted that the girl had thrown away her chances to gratify a minute's anger, but her hatred of her husband's relatives prompted her to openly approve Helen's spirited course.

'Seventeen years ago, Lady Grahame shut her house against me; to-day, she invites my child in order that she may be insulted. Gracious heaven! that I should have married into such a family!' exclaimed the injured matron with a withering glance at the innocent Mr. Vanstone.

'Do not say anything to wound papa. He cannot help his relatives' ill-breeding,' cried Helen quickly.

'You do not know, you cannot enter into my feelings, child,' said Mrs. Vanstone, with a severe look ; then after a pause she added, in the tone of one whose cup of bitterness is full,—'We are the victims of fate ; it is our destiny to lie down and be trampled in the mire. I would to heaven that I had never given birth to a child to inherit my wretched ill-fortune.'

At another time Helen's sense of humour would have prompted her to smile inwardly at her mother's melodramatic airs and phrases, but at the present moment all this chimed in with her own woe, and before she went to bed she had another good cry, in which exhausting pastime Mrs. Vanstone joined her.

And that was the end of the ball to which she had looked forward with such eagerness and pleasurable expectation, the ball at which she was to meet the Byronic and romantic young hero, who would shower love and riches on her, and lift her for ever out of this sordid existence. Alas for the illusions of youth! the disappointment she had experienced to-night was but a type of the disappointments that wait us through life, stealing the light from our eyes, the hope from our hearts, and peopling the past with bitter and mocking memories.

She sobbed herself softly to sleep, repeating many times under her breath that she was very miserable, and that life was hard, and cruel, and joyless. A man or woman of the world would have laughed at such trouble; but she was only a child and cursed with a sensitiveness that made her wound herself more deeply than the hand of others could wound her. In the years to come she learned to look upon this as the lightest grief she had ever known.

CHAPTER VI.

ENNUI.

LADY GRAHAME was a well-meaning, but at the same time haughty, woman with a strong sense of her own dignity. She considered that Helen had acted rudely and petulantly, and that it was her place to apologise. As our heroine could not be brought to this view, friendly relations were in consequence suspended. Lady Grahame occasionally came to Thomas Street to see her cousin, and on these occasions Helen generally contrived to be out of the way.

'I regret for her own sake that she has not more sense,' remarked the great lady, in discussing the subject with her husband.

'It is evident that although she resembles the Vanstones in appearance, she is a Tubbs by nature.'

As time rolled on, and the monotony of life in Thomas Street grew daily more irksome, Helen began to own to herself that she had acted rashly and foolishly in offending her rich relative, since it was only through her intervention that she could obtain an entrance into the bright world for which she so ardently pined. But pride prevented her from making the *amende honorable* which would have regained Lady Grahame's good-will, and by this obstinacy, she cut off from herself for the present, at least, all chance of seeing good society.

'Mamma, dear, I am dreadfully weary of this life,' she said one day to her mother. They had just returned from Regent Street, having indulged in the unwonted luxury of a long day's shopping ; and the sight of the carriages, the fine things in the windows, the gaily-dressed people, had filled the girl with a feeling of discontent not altogether unnatural in one so young, so beautiful, and so fitted by nature for a superior sphere.

Mrs. Vanstone shook her head with a mournful air. 'It is no use repining, my child. We are in the gutter, and in the gutter we shall remain.' When strongly moved, this worthy lady's expressions were more often remarkable for vigour than elegance.

'I have been thinking seriously of our situation, and I have an idea,' resumed Helen, after a pause. 'I lead a dreadfully useless life here, and I should like to do something, to turn any talents I may possess to advantage. It is terrible to go about the world as I do with hardly a shilling in my pocket.'

'Helen, I give you all the money I can. If you only knew how I have to manage and pinch—' ·

She interrupted her mother's expostulation by flinging her arms round her neck and kissing her fondly.

'You are the best, the dearest, the most self-sacrificing of mothers,' she cried gratefully ; 'but the utmost you can do is very little. Now, would it not be nice if I could earn money for myself, to give you and me a few luxuries that we should so appreciate.'

'What do you propose?' asked Mrs. Vanstone doubtfully.

'I had an idea of becoming an actress,' replied Helen, in a somewhat faltering voice.

Her mother started as if she had been shot. 'Good heavens, child, never mention such a thing to me again!' she cried fiercely. 'I would rather see you in your coffin than exposing youself to the gaze of every insolent fool who pays to stare at you.'

Helen sighed gently.

'What do you say to singing?'

'Very little better,' said Mrs. Vanstone gruffly. 'The idea of a Vanstone becoming a public singer!'

She hated her husband's relatives, but she could not forget that they had aristocratic blood in their veins, and that her daughter had inherited it.

'I could change my name,' put in the girl artfully. Mrs Vanstone did not reply, being apparently engaged in pursuing the train of thought conjured up by her daughter's proposition, and Helen continued,—

' Even if you disliked me to appear in
public, I could learn enough to enable me
to get a few pupils quietly. There would
be no degradation in that, and the money
would be a pleasant addition to our income.'

Mrs. Vanstone's face wore a dubious look.
' I will think over the matter, my dear, and
let you know.'

But Helen attacked her again the next
day ; and before a week was over, so per-
suasively had she argued, that her mother
was induced to give her consent to her
taking lessons with a view to becoming a
public singer.

' And if I haven't voice enough for that, I
can fall back upon the teaching,' urged the
girl.

Mrs. Vanstone gave her consent from
mixed motives. She saw Helen was terribly
tired of her monotonous life, and she thought
that taking lessons would at least give her
occupation, and distract her thoughts from
their sordid circumstances. The next difficulty to be encountered was in the choice of
a professor. But Helen was prepared with
all the details of her scheme, and immedi-

ately named Mr. Mountjoy Smith. Several distinguished artistes had received their preliminary training at the hands of this gentleman.

Mr. Mountjoy Smith resided in a medium-sized house in the neighbourhood of Blooms-bury. Mother and daughter made their way thither, and requested an interview with the professor.

He was a fine-looking man, with a noble-shaped head, surmounted by curly hair; a Roman profile, and a somewhat grand manner. He was none of your shabby, sloppy-looking Bohemians, but wore good clothes, showed a large expanse of shirt-front, and arranged his neck-tie with scrupulous neatness. In somewhat hesitating phrase, Helen explained the object of her visit. Mr. Mountjoy Smith listened with bland attention.

' I understand you perfectly,' he said, when she had finished. ' You wish first of all to ascertain whether you have a voice, and in case it proves that you do possess one, you desire to have it cultivated with a view to pecuniary profit.'

' Exactly,' replied Helen, greatly obliged to him for comprehending her so readily.

' Perhaps you will kindly sing me any song that shows your powers to the greatest advantage,' said the professor, walking towards the piano and opening it.

Helen felt terribly nervous at having to begin business so soon, but intimated that ' Robin Adair ' was generally considered her masterpiece.

In the twinkling of an eye, Mr. Mountjoy Smith had picked out a copy of the song from a pile of music, had seated himself at the stool, and struck the preliminary chords of the accompaniment.

' Now, if you please, and try and forget that there is anybody listening to you.'

Thus encouraged, she began in a somewhat faint voice ; but as she went on, her nervousness grew less, and she contrived to sing it, if not at her best, yet well enough to give him an idea of what she could do.

He rose, and said gravely,—' You have the pipes.' This phrase he repeated two or three times, as if by it he were better explaining his opinion to himself. Then he addressed the expectant performer,—

'Of course, the organ is very uncultivated, but it is mellow and sympathetic. Power would come in time ; and you have also good natural taste.'

Helen blushed vividly with pleasure and bashfulness. Delicious words they seemed to her, comforting, and symbolical of future triumph. In the golden days of youth, expectation is so much superior to reality. The first hope of drawing a prize in the lottery of life sends a fiercer thrill through our hearts than even the actual drawing of it. For, before that takes place, we have experienced the chills of doubt, delay, and despair.

After a little more talk about the voice and the mode of training, they came to the more difficult question of terms. Mr. Mountjoy Smith wanted a guinea a lesson, which, by degrees, he reduced to fifteen shillings. Poor Helen's face fell.

'It is more than I expected to give more than I could afford to give, in fact,' she explained to him, flushing sensitively under his gaze. 'Of course, if I were rich, I should not want to enter into this sort of thing at all.'

Mr. Smith considered. 'What sum had you fixed in your own mind?' he asked, after a pause.

'I thought half-a-guinea!' replied poor Helen, feeling very ashamed at having to beat down so grand a looking personage.

Mr. Smith considered further; then, with a burst of frankness, he cried, 'Well, then, we will say half-a-guinea a lesson, and two lessons a week.'

'Oh! thank you very much. I am sorry to be compelled to ask you to take less than your usual fee.'

The professor smiled kindly at her. He was a married man, with a large family, but he was not insensible to beauty, and he thought he had never seen a lovelier girl than this delicate, graceful, blushing young creature, who could only afford to give him half-a-guinea. Had she been a plain young woman, he might have refused to take her on such terms. Such is the way of the world,—a kind one to persons who fulfil its preconceived notions in various small matters, a hard one to those who cannot.

Then Helen, who was not a bad hand at business, in spite of her timidity, started another question.

' I want to ask you this, Mr. Smith. Assuming for a moment that my voice repays cultivation, and you think me competent to appear in public, could you help me to make a debût. In other words, could you launch me ?'

Mr. Smith considered for a moment or two. It did not seem a question quite so easy to answer as that about terms. After a pause, he replied,—

' Yes. I think I could guarantee that.' He added, with a grand manner that suited well with his fine figure and Roman profile,' —' Talent has seldom much difficulty in finding a market.'

This was a vague kind of sentiment that did not quite satisfy Helen, and she was about to pin the professor to some more definite statement, when Mrs. Vanstone struck in,—

'It is too soon to talk about that, my dear. Let us first wait and see how your voice turns out.'

Mr. Mountjoy Smith looked relieved. 'That would be the best plan,' he added, with a resumption of his grand manner. 'Should our hopes in that respect be realised, there would be little difficulty in coming to an understanding on the other matter.' This meant, of course, that he would require a large share out of her earnings; but neither Helen nor her mother suspected it, not being versed in the ways of professors *et hoc genus omne.* The only doubt that his hesitating manner raised in the girl's mind, was whether he had the influence necessary to launch her.

Mother and daughter walked on in silence for some little time after they emerged from Mr. Smith's somewhat dingy house. Then all at once Helen cried bluntly,—'Mamma, do you think him a humbug ?'

Mrs. Vanstone often used words herself that would not pass muster in the best circles, but she was careful that her daughter should not so derogate, so she observed rather severely, ' My dear, that is not a nice word.'

' Of course it isn't,' said Helen, with a merry smile ; 'but you know, dear, it is so delightfully expressive. And I must confess that there is something in Mr. Mountjoy Smith's whole manner, handsome looking man as he is, that seems to exactly suit the term. He is too suave.'

' Perhaps that comes from his mixing so much with women. At any rate, I observed him pretty closely, and I did not come to the conclusion that he was a greater scoundrel than the majority of men. I daresay he is a brute in his own home.' Mrs. Vanstone was a virulent man-hater, and held firmly to her theory that all men are by nature tyrannical, brutal, and hypocritical.

' I am sorry for Mrs. Mountjoy if such is the case,' replied Helen, laughing ; ' but I must confess I was not studying him with a view to his domestic character, but as to his ability to do what I want with him.'

' Humph ! that you must take your

chance of. We know nothing about this
kind of people. All we know generally
is that the world is full of rogues, who
are only too glad to pick your pocket in
a genteel kind of way,' said her mother
gruffly.

'It would be a terrible thing to pay
our money and do no good by it,' cried
poor Helen, with a twinge of conscience ;
adding, in a more cheerful tone, 'But
after a month's trial of this gentleman, we
shall be better able to form an opinion.'

Mrs. Vanstone said nothing. There are
wheels within wheels, and she was not at
all ambitious that her daughter should
degrade herself by singing in public.

CHAPTER VII.

THE BEAUFORTS.

ELEN began her lessons with Mr. Smith, and made the house in Thomas Street musical with the daily practice of exercises, shakes, and trills. Mrs. Vanstone found the noise somewhat irritating, but she made no complaint. The girl was occupied, and taken out of herself and the region of melancholy thoughts ; and so far this was desirable.

One day she returned from the professor's in a high state of excitement, eyes sparkling, lips quivering with eagerness to tell her adventure.

'Oh, mamma dear, I have met such a delightful girl at Mr. Smith's—a Miss Florence Beaufort. She is going to appear in public soon, and Mr. Smith thought we might try a few duets together. Is it not strange ? her family has come down in the world like us. Her father is most respectably connected. Sir Rupert Beaufort, who commanded the expedition against the Wallaboos, is one brother, and Dr. Beaufort of Curzon Street, Mayfair, is another. But they look down upon him, of course, as is the way with rich relations.'

Here she paused to take breath ; and Mrs. Vanstone, who began to feel a little interested herself, enquired, ' What does he do for a living ? '

' He is an actor, but I am afraid does not do much. One daughter teaches music, their only son is in a bank, and Florence, as I told you, will shortly earn her living as a professional. Oh, she is such a dear girl,—so natural, so pleasant, not a bit of false pride.'

' She seems at least a communicative young lady, to have told you her family history so soon. Pray where was all this related,—before Smith ? '

' Oh, no,' replied Helen quickly, feeling

anxious that her new friend should appear to advantage in her mother's eyes. 'We walked part of the way home together. She lives at St. John's Wood. I do so long for next Thursday, when we are going to sing some more duets together.'

Thursday came in due course, and the two young ladies met again in the professor's room. As he was not yet come in, Miss Beaufort favoured her fellow pupil with some more of the family history; and Helen, won by such artless candour, communicated a little of their own misfortunes. The fair Florence listened with a sympathising air, and when she had finished, said sweetly, 'We are companions in affliction, why should we not be dear friends?'

Moved by a common impulse, the two girls embraced tenderly. When they withdrew gently from each other's arms, the eyes of both were moist. It was a touching sight; touching to anybody except a hardened cynic, who would have sworn that six months hence they would not have a kind word to say of each other. After the duets had been gone through, they walked home together. As they bade each other adieu at the corner of the street where they took separate ways, Miss Beaufort said in a persuasive tone,—

'Will you come and see me? You will find us but poor, broken-down folks, it is true, but we are *not* poor in mental resources.'

'I shall be delighted,' replied Helen, colouring with pleasure at the prospect of making the acquaintance of so charming a family.

'Say, then, to-morrow at six. Once we could have asked you to dinner, but now I can only say come to tea.'

Helen replied gracefully that it would afford her exquisite pleasure to partake of that humble meal in Miss Beaufort's company, and they parted with mutual satisfaction.

The next day she set out for St. John's Wood in a condition of high delight. Poor child! going into society of any kind was a novelty to her. Mrs. Vanstone had wished to array her in her best, but Helen had pointed out that good taste required, she should make her first visit dressed as plainly as possible. 'You know, mamma, they are poor people, and to put on grand things might appear like an insult to their poverty,' she said.

This was all very right, of course, and showed a delicate feeling on her part; but she was fairly surprised to find the Beaufort family decked out with a splendour that put her own raiment completely in the shade. Mrs. Beaufort, a majestic-looking woman, appeared imposing in a rich silk dress, and an artistic head-dress, with a very fine feather. Miss Beaufort, the teacher, was in pink. Florence, who was rather a pretty girl, looked captivating in blue. Mr. Beaufort, a handsome man about six feet high, had on morning dress, and Helen thought his coat must have been cut by no ordinary artist.

Mrs. Beaufort received her with a stately courtesy. Mr. Beaufort bade her welcome in a more hearty fashion.

'Charmed to make your acquaintance, my dear young lady.' He paused for a second, and then added, with a theatrical

kind of sigh,—'My daughter tells me that
you too have known misfortune. I need,
therefore, make no apology for receiving
you in a home so little suited to the tastes
and aspirations of either of us.'

This was all very grand and imposing,
but, as Helen thought, hardly in the best
taste. But her closer acquaintance with
Mr. Beaufort convinced her that he took
a positive delight in dwelling upon his
misfortunes, and a still keener delight in
talking about his family. After a little
time spent in general conversation, they
went down to tea, Mr. Beaufort escort-
ing Helen to the dining-room with the
air of a man accustomed to the best
society.

'My brother, Sir Rupert, dines at a
grand banquet given by the commander-
in-chief to-night, while I am eating bread
and butter in a humble cottage in St.
John's Wood,' said the broken-down gentleman, in the course of the meal : he added
with a sigh—'And yet we are sons of the
same father.'

'Thank Heaven there will be no rich

and poor in the next world,' said the majestic Mrs. Beaufort with an emphasis that made the feather in her head - dress shake.

Helen glanced at the speaker with some curiosity. She was a very grand-looking personage, and all the family seemed to treat her with great deference. The only thing that puzzled the girl was that while she had heard all about the Beaufort's down to the ninety-ninth cousin, she had never heard a word about the mother's family.

Tea proceeded slowly, in consequence of the chat, and Mr. Beaufort took every opportunity of slipping in something about 'Sir Rupert!' He never spoke of him simply as my brother; it was always the same phrase, 'My brother Sir Rupert,' as if he loved the flavour of the title, *e.g.*, 'When I was in Edinburgh with my brother Sir Rupert — as I was walking down Bond Street with my brother, Sir Rupert,' etc., etc.

In the evening they had music, playing and singing, and Mr. Beaufort contributed to the general amusement by recitation.

He chose Antony's oration, and 'To be or not to be;' and after she had heard these, Helen no longer wondered that he did not succeed in his profession. A more monotonous or lugubrious delivery it was impossible to conceive. As a performance, it was infinitely below the average of penny readings. But his family evidently thought him a fine reciter, and applauded vigorously; and Helen, not to be behindhand in politeness, did the same.

'I'll give you Gray's Elegy,' said the would-be actor, stimulated by the applause. And through that not very cheerful poem he drawled in the same monotonous tone, and with the same monotonous see-saw action of the hand, which was the only approach he made towards action. When he had concluded, he said in his ordinary voice, which was a cheerful one,—'I used to recite that when a boy at my father's parties. It was my brother Sir Rupert's favourite piece. I little thought I should have to come to that sort of thing for a living.'

Helen looked sympathising, but had a melancholy conviction that the audience was yet to be found who would give a penny for a recitation of this kind. But, taken as a whole, the evening passed very pleasantly, and she felt sorry when it was time to go.

Mrs. Beaufort kissed her affectionately, and intimated that she should be glad to make the acquaintance of Mrs. Vanstone. 'My wretched health prevents me from going out, but I should be very pleased to see her here if she can put up with a dull evening. We have at least misfortunes in common.'

Then Florence, who was a business-like young lady, added,—'General invitations are no use, nobody knows when to come. Let Helen appoint an evening, when she will bring her mother.' There was a chorus of approval from the whole family at this proposal, and being so hard pressed, Helen suggested that day fortnight. But it seemed that the ardour of the Beauforts to make Mrs. Vanstone's acquaintance could not brook so long a delay, and it was eventually decided that they should meet that day week.

When Helen informed her mother of the invitation she had accepted for her, Mrs. Vanstone at first pished and frowned, and said she did not want to go gadding about at her time of life. When, however, the day came round, she arrayed herself in her best, and sallied forth with her daughter to St. John's Wood.

Florence and Mr. Beaufort received them in the hall, and escorted them to the drawing-room, where Mrs. Beaufort was waiting in state to receive them. And then, as the eyes of the two mothers met, a most extraordinary thing happened. A vivid carnation slowly spread over Mrs. Beaufort's face, and instead of her usual majestic appearance, there was visible an air of mortification and embarrassment. On her side, Mrs. Vanstone looked equally embarrassed, but a trifle less ashamed. Being the more self-possessed of the two she was the first to speak.

'Am I mistaken ; or do I see again my old acquaintance, Jemima Scroggs ?' she said, wonderingly.

'You do ; and you are Martha Tubbs,'

replied the other lady, advancing with an awkward air of cordiality. They then embraced, wishing each other at the bottom of the sea all the time.

It was an embarrassing scene to more than the two principal actors in it. Helen was not in the least ashamed of her mother's origin, and bore herself bravely; but Mr. Beaufort and the girls had faces like scarlet. After all this boasting about the family, and the constant references to ' My brother Sir Rupert,' it was very mortifying to think that Helen should know the humble antecedents of the mother.

Miss Jemima Scroggs was the daughter of a Slocombe publican, and in her youth had been the playmate of Martha Tubbs. This young lady had rather looked down upon Jemima, and entertained for her much the kind of feeling which a piece of silk, supposing it to be gifted with a delicate sense of social distinction, might be imagined to exhibit towards a pewter pot. Mr. Scroggs had failed and gone to London, so that neither of the girls had become acquainted with the after history of the other until they met on this occasion, under the names of Mrs. Beaufort and Mrs. Vanstone.

In the course of the evening the embarrassment wore off, and the two matrons chatted about old times. Even Florence, who had looked the most mortified of the family, recovered herself so far as to whisper gushingly to Helen, 'How strangely things come about in this world! To think that your mother should be an old friend of mine. This constitutes another link between us, darling.' And the warm-hearted creature kissed her friend affectionately.

Mrs. Vanstone was nothing if not critical, and when she and her daughter were beyond the hearing of the Beauforts, who had clustered in a family group at the door, her first words were,—

'How in the name of wonder do those people live? Did you ever see such a sight as that foolish old woman (thus disrespectfully did she designate the friend of her youth) with her feathers and lace, as if she were in a Belgravian drawing-room? And she only a publican's daughter, too. As for that poor noodle Beaufort, he surely cannot earn a penny with that horrid sing-song voice of his. He calls himself an actor; where did he ever act?'

'I don't think he has performed in London,' replied Helen shortly. She did not quite relish her mother's unflattering comments.

'I should doubt if he would be allowed to perform at a fair,' said Mrs. Vanstone, in her most contemptuous manner.

'But Florence is a charming girl,' pleaded Helen.

'I don't take to her, my dear. Plenty to say, very gushing, and all that sort of thing; but, in my opinion, decidedly sly. You don't look below the surface.'

'Oh, mamma, how can you say so? She is artlessness itself,' rejoined Helen warmly.

'Pooh! that's all put on, I tell you.' Then returning to her old enquiry,—'I should very much like to know how they live. They say they are as poor as church mice; then where does that old Jemima get her feathers and silks from?'

This mystery so weighed upon Mrs. Vanstone's mind, that she communicated it to

her husband, who was soon in a position
to solve it. At his club he met a man
who knew all the Beauforts, and was perfectly ready to tell all he knew.

'Beaufort an actor, sir?' cried the communicative personage : 'No more an actor
than you are. How do they live ? simply
by cadging, there is no other word for it.
He cadges, the old woman cadges, the girls
cadge. I know a man now, sir, that they've
got over three hundred pounds out of at
different times. I lent the old sinner twenty
pounds once myself to stave off an execution ; and be-gad, not content with never
repaying me, he actually called on me a
month after and requested another loan !
Cool, eh ? He is fertile in resources, and
can dress up any number of plausible lies.'

'But how does he contrive to always find
people who will lend. I don't know where
I could go for five pounds, much less three
hundred ?' asked Mr. Vanstone, wonderingly.

'Luck, sir ; sheer luck. The family, who
are really respectable, cut him on his marriage. Mrs. B. was a publican's daughter,
you know. He was then in a fairly flourish-

ing way of business as a wine merchant.
But the most unbounded extravagance and
idleness made him a bankrupt. He turned
his attention to acting ; but he never got
more than one engagement, to play Polonius,
at the Margate Theatre, and that was only
for a week. Being a plausible fellow, he
managed to get a lot of friends, and he
has lived on them ever since. When they
are tired of listening to him, he sends the
girls to cry to them.'

It was evident from this graphic description that Mr. Beaufort belonged to that class
of men whose moral vision is so oblique, and
who are so steeped in vice, that they are at
all times unscrupulous and aggressive. Yet
they seem to pass to a certain extent un-
scathed through all sorts of troubles ; their
life being an alternation of squalor and
luxury. There are not a few of these gay
Bohemians, of a cleverer type than the
Beauforts, who may be seen driving through
the London streets in a smart brougham
with a high stepper, while there is an
execution in the house for a few pounds
owed to some tradesman. Nay, they look

as flourishing as ever, even after they have been made bankrupts, and their assets represented by a cipher.

They dress well, have very loud trappings on their persons in the shape of jewels, live like fighting cocks, run into debt anywhere and everywhere, pass now and then a few hours of quiet contemplation in prison, and play hide and seek with the sheriff's minions. Eternally in debt, and eternally compounding with their creditors, they thus manage to keep on 'pegging away.' Begging letters are with such men a lucrative branch of polite art. Their three chief canons for guidance are comprised in borrowing, eating, drinking, and making a good appearance, and never repaying. These maxims, like some of the physical laws, reduce things to a state of equilibrium, so that it may be said, they live to borrow, and borrow to live.

Those who know the world well, and have studied this class of men, must declare that they are rascals, at once unscrupulous, truculent, servile, insolent, and mendacious, especially the *bon vivant* section, who are dangerous from their plausibility and suave speech, and who spend as much on eating and drinking in a day as would keep a more honest man for a month.

Mr. Vanstone returned home, primed with this history. His wife did not look exactly pleased; but there was about her that air of passive content, with which, according to a cynical philosopher, some people take the misfortunes of their friends. Helen was very crestfallen, there being a terrible air of truth about it all.

'Well, thank heaven, I don't buy feathers and lace with other persons' money!' said Mrs. Vanstone at length. It was astonishing how that gorgeous head-dress seemed to rankle in her mind. 'But Jemima was always unprincipled when a girl; always took more than her share of buns and tarts; and old Scroggs cheated a lot of people in Slocombe.'

'Poor things! we don't know what we should be driven to if we had not a penny of our own,' put in Helen, with sweet womanly pity.

'I am quite sure I should never degrade

myself by living on the charity of others,'
replied her mother grimly ; and, to do her
justice, she would not have condescended
to the mean shifts of the Beauforts.

The knowledge of their history did not,
however, make any apparent difference in
the relations between the two families. It
was still 'Florence dear !' and 'Helen
darling !' with the girls, while the elder ladies
Martha'd and Jemima'd each other with a
great appearance of cordiality. Mr. Vanstone was also introduced in due time, and
the Misses Beaufort declared they had fallen
in love with him, a circumstance that made
the old gentleman feel flattered, and his
wife suspicious.

'I know that Florence is an artful minx !'
said Mrs. Vanstone, in her usual uncompromising manner.

Time proved her estimate of Miss Beaufort's character correct. One evening Mr.
Vanstone, on returning from his club, put
into his wife's hand a letter which had
been addressed to him there. It proved
to be from the artless Florence, and Mrs.
Vanstone perused it with a frowning brow.

It contained a request for a loan of fifty pounds, to be repaid out of her earnings as soon as she appeared in public. Its conclusion was as follows,—' Please do not let Mrs. Vanstone or darling Helen know anything of this.'

Mrs. Vanstone threw down the note in a furious passion. It was well for Florence that she was not behind the door, for she would have heard some unpleasant truths of herself. Even Helen, unsuspicious as she was by nature, had her eyes opened at last. She burst into tears, and cried in a broken-hearted voice,—

' Oh, what a hateful world this is ! To think that we were only invited there and treated so kindly in the hope of being made use of. I shall never believe anybody after this ; and I had grown to love that girl like a sister.'

Mrs. Vanstone undertook to answer the letter, and wrote what she called a ' trimmer.' Miss Florence did not condescend to hold further communication with the elder lady, but she sent a freezingly polite note to Helen, in which she intimated that her mother's insulting and outrageous conduct had rendered it impossible to continue her acquaintance with any member of the Vanstone family.

Thus ended this little friendship ; and as Helen did not make the progress that she expected under the tuition of Mr. Mountjoy Smith, and began to have an uneasy suspicion that he was somewhat of a charlatan, she abandoned the idea of a public career, and avoided a house where she was likely to come into contact with the false Florence.

But life seemed to be duller than ever in Thomas Street, with no friend, and no hope of getting into anything better.

'The world is a dreary dwelling place, mamma!' she said as they sat together one evening, trying to kill the time with fancy work. 'I wish a diversion of some kind would happen.'

As she spoke, there came a knock at the street door. She ran to open it, thinking it was her father. When she came to reflect afterwards, she said to herself that this knock had come as an answer to her wish.

CHAPTER VIII.

A VISITOR.

GREAT was Helen's vexation, when on opening the street door, the tall figure of a stranger presented itself to her view in place of the familiar form of her father. Her vexation, however, did not prevent her from noting that this stranger was young, had dark eyes and hair, clear cut features, and the air of a gentleman.

'Is Mr. Vanstone at home?' He had begun his question in what must have been his habitual voice, which was rather hard and sharp—the voice of a man who is somewhat stern and peremptory by temperament, but on perceiving that the person who had performed this menial office was a girl, whose marvellous beauty and refined bearing he recognised at a glance, it took a courteous inflection.

'No, he is not,' replied Helen, curtly and sharply. The courtesy in his tone increased her vexation, for it showed that if he was acquainted with her father, as he seemed to be, her identity was not to be concealed from him.

But the repellant tones did not seem to affect this young man's appreciation of her beauty, for his glance dwelt upon her with an admiration that he found it impossible to repress, and self-possessed as was Helen on ordinary occasions, she felt herself blushing furiously beneath the gaze of those dark, eloquent eyes, that seemed to look into her very heart.

He perceived her confusion, and remembered that he was not acting a very gentlemanly part, by staring at a young lady till he brought the blood to her cheek, and he indirectly apologised for his rudeness by resuming the parley in a voice that was almost humble.

'I am very sorry to have to trouble you

with any more questions, but I should be glad to know if he is likely to be in shortly. I wish to see him very particularly, and as my home is a long distance from here, I should prefer to return with my mission achieved.'

Whether it was that his anxious desire to apologise for his rudeness softened Helen's asperity, or that her female instincts whispered to her she was already the object of an admiration very intense, and out of mere coquetry she was not averse to fascinate him more deeply, certain it is that her vexation disappeared as if by magic, and when she answered him, it was with one of the most charming smiles in the world.

'It is no trouble to answer so simple a question as that. I expect papa in every moment, in fact, I took your knock for his. Would you like to come in and wait? He cannot possibly be long.'

The young stranger accepted the invitation with an eagerness that was flattering enough to the girl, who in a few seconds had made so powerful an impression upon him. His politeness prompted him to shut the door for her.

'And now it is time that I should make myself known,' he said, as they stood together in the hall, very dimly lighted by a flicker of gas in a somewhat dirty lamp. ' My name is Weldon—Ralph Weldon—and I belong to the same club as your father.'

Mrs. Vanstone, on hearing the sound of voices in such close proximity, advanced to the door of the dining-room, and put her head out to see what was going on. She was not particularly reassured when she perceived a tall young man standing bareheaded by her daughter's side. It was just possible that he might have designs upon the coats.

' Helen, who is there ? ' she called out, sharply.

Helen made Mr. Weldon a sign to follow her into the dining-room, where she explained matters succinctly to her mother.

' This gentleman is Mr. Weldon, mamma, a member of papa's club ; and as he wishes to see him very particularly, I have asked him to wait a little while.'

Mrs. Vanstone gave a sort of half bow, which might be taken to mean both assent to her daughter's proposition and an acknowledgement of the young man's presence. Mr. Ralph Weldon also bowed on his side ; and as he did so their eyes met. In that swift interchange of glances each conceived a dislike to the other, a perfectly groundless but at the same time invincible repugnance, that was never conquered in the months and years of their after intercourse.

They all sat down ; and those dark, earnest eyes, under whose gaze the unaccustomed blood had rushed so swiftly to Helen's cheek, sought her own, as if compelled by some powerful instinct which their possessor could not control. In those long and ardent glances he took in every detail of her faultless beauty ; the smooth, white forehead, shaded by the glossy, abundant hair ; the liquid brown eyes, that seemed to light up the room with their thrilling glance ; the exquisitely-curved coral lips, through which gleamed the brilliant teeth ; the small, delicate-shaped ears ; the lithe and supple figure ;—all those details which made her seem the fairest woman he had ever gazed upon.

It is customary to ridicule the idea of love
at first sight; but experience tells us that a
glance, a tone, may plant in the heart the
seed that time ripens into a blooming and
fragrant flower. Certain it is that Ralph
Weldon, a man over whose youth and childhood had rested the shadows of deep
sorrows, that had made life less bright to him
than to most; whose pulse had never yet
thrilled at a woman's voice; whose heart
had never yet melted beneath the magic of
a woman's smile; who had grown to think
that the curse of joylessness, breathed upon
his childhood by the faults and the sufferings
of others, would cling to him and dog him
to the grave; who had learned to repay to
the world the hardness and scorn that he
had received from it,—certain it is, that
from the moment his glance had met the
glance of Helen Vanstone, as she stood in
that dimly lighted hall, he had seemed to
feel that a marvellous change was being
wrought in him.

For as he sat and watched the lights and
shadows that danced across her fair cheek,
the light that trembled in those sweet eyes,

such clear mirrors of the soul that they interpreted, he began to think that the world was not so dark, so hard, or so scornful, but that a woman like this could illumine it with her love, and take away the sting from its scorn. He had never yet thought seriously about love ; his narrow circumstances had precluded him from mingling with women of refined mind and manners, and he had nothing but contempt for those mindless, half-educated girls, who, with the exception of his dead mother and sister, had made up his whole experience of the fairer portion of creation.

But here, in a soil as uncongenial as could well be imagined, he saw that there flourished a flower of rare beauty and perfume ; and he gazed and marvelled, knowing but little of Gabriel Vanstone's past, as a man might gaze and marvel who finds a splendid and flawless diamond enshrined in a mean and paltry setting. And as the sordidness of the setting brings into greater relief the brilliance of the stone, so did this dingy home, with its dark and gloomy surroundings, enhance the charms of this radiant girl,

on whom nature and education had stamped
the impress of gentlewoman. For although
Helen had not escaped the taint of Bohemianism, as how was it possible she should
have done—her Bohemianism was rather of
that kind which springs from a certain lawlessness of spirit, from the constant warring
of the heart against the hateful conditions of
the life amid which it beats, than from the
innate vulgarity of a nature that deliberately
prefers coarseness to elegance, the common
to the refined.

In her quick and often petulant phrases,
he detected much that enabled him to guess
the conditions of her life. It was easy to
discover from them that she was discontented with her surroundings. And, taking
all that he had been able to perceive of the
street and the house, into consideration,
Mr. Weldon was not surprised that such
was the case. At the club, he had heard
something about old Vanstone having once
been a rich man, and having lost his money
in some unfortunate speculation, and the
refined bearing of this young girl bore out
the fact. No wonder that she felt herself

out of place here, he said to himself,—her beauty would have adorned a palace.

Feeling it incumbent upon himself to find some topics of conversation, he asked her if she had been to any of the theatres lately. Fortunately, she had been to two, so she was enabled to discuss the merits of the pieces she had seen with her visitor, who appeared to frequent every theatre in the metropolis.

' Why, you have seen everything !' she cried, after Mr. Weldon had described all the plots, and criticised all the actors and actresses.

' I can get orders whenever I want, you know,' he said.

' Oh ! how nice. Papa knows two or three actors, but he never gets any. I suppose he is too shy to ask for them.'

' Will you allow me to send you some ?' said Mr. Weldon, politely. It is distressing to have to record that this offer did not proceed from pure philanthropy, as the astute reader will have guessed already. The artful fellow wanted to get an excuse for creeping into the house, and he fore-

saw some difficulty in the matter, for
Mrs. Vanstone was one of the dragon
species.

'Oh, I should be so grateful! Mamma
and I lead a very lonely life, and a visit to
a theatre or a concert is our only dissipation.
We have no nice clubs like you fortunate
men.'

'That is only a matter of time,' replied
Mr. Weldon, smiling. 'Only the other day
I received a prospectus of one which is
to admit both sexes. In a few years,
perhaps months, we shall get to one for
ladies exclusively; but I don't think it will
answer.'

'You mean they'll quarrel till there's not
a member left,' cried Helen, merrily. 'But
I don't agree with you, Mr. Weldon. I
think if the men are rigorously excluded,
they will get on very well. It is the intro-
duction of your sex that makes the ladies
quarrelsome.'

'Of course I bow to your superior judgment, and feel how profoundly ignorant I am
on such matters. The fact is, I have
a .very small acquaintance among the fair

sex; hence my want of knowledge,' was Mr. Weldon's answer.

There was silence for a little time after this, which was employed by Helen in guessing at the profession of their visitor. One thing was very clear, he was a gentleman. He did not look like a City man, at least not like such City men as started from Thomas Street in the morning. He was not prim enough for a lawyer, and he looked many stages above a clerk. He certainly was not a doctor, neither had he the appearance of a military man. In Helen's private opinion, he more resembled the exquisites she had seen at Lady Grahame's than any other class with which she was acquainted; but it was hardly possible that he would be a friend of her papa's, and come to Thomas Street, if he were very fashionable. After having exhausted probabilities and possibilities, she was reluctantly obliged to come to the conclusion that he must be a young man of no social status.

'Do you go to the exhibition of pictures, Miss Vanstone?' he asked suddenly, in the midst of her musings.

She answered in the affirmative; and this led to a discussion on art and things artistic, in which he displayed so much knowledge, that she had now little doubt as to his profession. In order to be certain on the point, she put a leading question. 'You seem to be wonderfully well-informed in these matters, Mr. Weldon?'

'I ought to be,—I am an artist,' he answered.

'Dear me, I should never have taken you for one,' said Helen, innocently.

'May I ask your reasons?' asked Mr. Weldon, smiling.

She blushed, and would have avoided giving an answer, but he pressed her.

Now, please, Miss Vanstone, do not be afraid of giving offence. I should like to hear a little truth about my own profession, at least glean an idea of the impression they make upon other people.'

Thus exhorted, Helen pocketed her fears, and said laughingly,—

'Well, I have always understood that artists are a somewhat slovenly and untidy-looking race, with long hair and ill-fitting clothes. Now you, on the contrary, look as if you had prepared yourself for a promenade down Bond Street or some other centre of fashion.'

It was Ralph Weldon's turn to blush a little at this compliment. 'Certainly, I never thought that genius was incompatible with neatness,' he answered. 'The world of Bohemia conforms more to convention than it used, Miss Vanstone. A poet of the Victorian era can enter a drawing-room without his " eye in fine frenzy rolling." '

' I should think all these kinds of professions,—poets, artists, and writers, were very unprofitable,' suddenly called out Mrs. Vanstone, in the intervals of her sewing. It was almost the first remark she had condescended to make, and Helen blushed vividly at its rudeness. She stole a glance at the visitor, and saw a burning spot on his cheek that told he felt it.

' May I ask whether you have known many who pursue these callings ?' he asked, coldly.

' No ; but I have heard and read a good deal about them. There was one man who poisoned himself in a garret, I forget his name ; and another who died through eating a crust which had been given him when he was starving.'

'I am encouraged to persevere in my profession by the remembrance that neither of these unfortunate men was an artist,' replied Weldon, sarcastically.

Now it must not be supposed that Mrs. Vanstone was so excessively ignorant as not to know she had been guilty of great coarseness and ill-breeding ; but the fact was, she had taken a dislike to this young man, and she was rather pleased to annoy him.

The slight embarrassment that resulted from this brief passage caused Mr. Weldon to glance at the clock, and to express his regret at detaining them.

Helen smiled, and replied with the frankness that is born of a Bohemian existence,— ' You are not detaining us at all.   Our life is so monotonous, that the advent of a chance visitor like yourself is quite a sensation. Mamma and I get very tired of each other's company sometimes, and our friends can be counted upon our fingers.'

Mrs. Vanstone gave a slight frown, to express disapproval of her daughter's candour. There was no necessity to let this young man know their affairs. But although Helen read its meaning, she did not choose to regard it, but continued her revelations.

'Of course we could make plenty of acquaintance if we liked, but then most of the people who are in the same position in point of wealth, or rather in the absence of it, as ourselves, are not to our tastes. That is the misfortune of having tastes beyond your means, Mr. Weldon.'

He knew that feeling well enough. ' I have often thought, Miss Vanstone, that it must be a great happiness to possess a nature which soon accommodates itself to its surroundings,' he added. ' In London you are at any rate free from the annoyance of having your neighbour's friendship forced upon you. In the country, you have hardly got in before you perceive that an obtrusively genial member of the family next door is lying in wait for you in the back or front garden.'

'Pray don't speak of neighbours,' replied Helen, with a vivacity that rendered her very charming. 'On our left there lives a poor, threadbare-looking man, who is a lawyer, I believe. How I pity him as I see him trudging every morning to business; for you know, Mr. Weldon, he has a dreadful *half-fed* look, that depresses me fearfully. And his wife, poor creature, she must have been a remarkably pretty girl, but now she has degenerated into a *drudge*. I catch glimpses of her in the garden occasionally, with a mysterious *dustery*-looking head-gear; and the children, their name is of course legion, have a broken-down appearance, horribly large feet and hands, as if their misfortunes had taken the form of elongating their extremities,—and the eldest boy, he cannot be more than sixteen, goes to business, and never gets back before eight. After his tea, poor fellow, he soothes himself by playing the concertina: you will hear him in a few minutes; he is very regular.'

Mr. Ralph Weldon smiled at her description, and replied,—'As far as my limited impressions would allow me to form a judgment, I should not consider this street a very cheerful abode. As your father does not actively follow any profession, I wonder you don't live in the country.'

' I suppose habit makes us keep here,' said Helen ; and then she added, with a very vivid blush, as if she felt too late the impropriety of what she was saying,—' And, moreover, moving is expensive, when one is not rich.'

This was more than Mrs. Vanstone could well stand.

' My dear Helen, this gentleman cannot possibly be interested in the paltry details with which you are furnishing him.'

She blushed yet a deeper red at her mother's rebuke, for she felt that it was not undeserved ; that she had let her tongue run too fast. Mr. Weldon came to the rescue by changing the conversation.

' I lead a very quiet life myself. My sister lives with me, and she is my great companion. Our friends can be counted, like your own, upon the fingers, so we fall back chiefly upon books for amusement.'

'You have a sister; how delightful that must be!' cried Helen, eagerly. 'How I wish that I had a brother!' She paused a second, then added in a more thoughtful tone, and unheedful of the rebuke which her mother had just administered,—'But, under the circumstances, perhaps it is better as it is. Men degenerate sooner than women, and my brother might have been like one of the boys next door, with large feet and great red hands. I couldn't have been fond of him then.'

'You could only love an Apollo, I suppose,' said Mr. Weldon, somewhat sarcastically.

'O dear, no! I have no predilection for handsome men; but I could *not* like anybody who was common, not a gentleman. You know, Mr. Weldon, poverty is not incompatible with refinement.'

'I flatter myself I am a proof of it in my own person,' he cried, laughing. What he admired intensely about this girl was her audacious frankness, and her fearless contempt for anything like sham. She hated her poverty, but she was not ashamed of it.

'I should like very much to be rich,' she said, after a pause.

'So would everybody, I think,' added Mr. Weldon, smiling at her emphasis.

'But I don't merely wish it because it would promote my own individual comfort, although that is its greatest consideration, but because it would give me the chance of snubbing a few people I know.'

A deep flush dyed the beautiful cheeks, and such a glittering light came into the dark brown eyes, as she followed out the rest of the picture.

'Oh, I would pay them all I owed with such heavy interest. I would sting them with my satire, and torture them with my insolence.'

Then all at once her vindictive mood changed, and she laughed merrily, as she cried, 'Heigho!—I shall never have an opportunity of exhibiting these Christian sentiments. I was born poor, and I shall die poor.'

As she indulged in this cheerful reflection, a knock was heard at the street door. She turned to the visitor and said,—

' That is papa ; you have not waited in vain.'

But Mr. Ralph Weldon would have preferred in his secret heart that he should have waited an hour or two more in her dear company.

CHAPTER IX.

DOMESTIC AMENITIES.

MR. GABRIEL VANSTONE was a tall, thin man, with small, meagre features, that expressed neither greatness of character nor strength of intellect. His eyes were small, and had the habit common to timid and insincere souls, of avoiding the gaze of others. His clothes, without being absolutely shabby, bore witness to good wear and constant brushing. But although insignificant in face and slender in form, he had the refined bearing of a gentleman ; and had you seen him amid surroundings superior to the present, you would not have concluded that he was not in perfect harmony with them. But in juxtaposition with the general dingi-

ness of life in Thomas Street, his well-worn
clothes, his conscious air, the irresolution
expressed in speech and gait, proclaimed him
at a glance one of the victims of fortune.
Never strong or resolute by temperament,
his pecuniary disasters, and the domestic
tyranny of his wife, had reduced him to a
feeble old man. In the presence of Mrs.
Vanstone he was apt to assume the air of a
naughty child, who expects to be chid for
his misconduct, and seems anxious to sneak
away from the coming storm. As soon as
he saw Ralph Weldon he gave a start,
which did not escape the keen eyes of his
wife, and advanced towards him, holding
out his hand with an awkward affectation
of cordiality.

'I wished to have a few moments' conversation with you, Mr. Vanstone,' said
Ralph, in his clear, ringing tones. His
keen eye read much of the state of affairs
between husband and wife, and he felt a
sovereign contempt for his acquaintance.
He did not as yet know the power of Mrs.
Vanstone's will, still less did he dream that
one day it would subjugate even him.

The mistress of the house addressed her lord (?) in a voice of much severity. 'We will leave you gentlemen together to talk over your *important* matters ; there is no fire in your study.' The emphasis laid on two or three of the words indicated her resentment at finding that Mr. Vanstone had any secrets, business or otherwise, with which she was unacquainted.

So great was Ralph Weldon's aversion to her, that he would have allowed her to remain in the cold half the night, but he could not tolerate the idea of turning sweet Helen out of the warm room.

' I must beg, Mrs. Vanstone, that we suffer the inconvenience, if any. I am the intruder, and what I have to say to your husband will not take five minutes. Let us go into any other apartment.'

'Will you follow me, please,' said the master of the house, in his feeble tones, desirous of ending a contest which might more embitter his spouse's temper. The unhappy man would shortly have to meet her in their common chamber.

When they were gone, Mrs. Vanstone let loose the floodgates of her soul.

'This is the way in which wives are treated. Men drag us down to poverty, they convert us into drudges, rob us of our looks and health, and then, greatest and deepest wrong of all, withhold their confidence from us.'

This pathetic lament was too much for Helen's gravity: she indulged in a peal of hearty laughter. 'O mamma, mamma, what a pity you were born without a touch of humour, you would have enjoyed such fun out of yourself. If you only knew how absurd all this sounds to a disinterested person. To hear you talk, anybody would think poor papa was a second Bluebeard, whereas his only crime is being very weak. O, my dear mother, please don't look so tragic!' cried the girl, with a second irrepressible fit of laughter as she saw that the injured woman was preparing to reply.

'Helen, your jesting is ill-timed ; you are too frivolous to understand my feelings. Nobody but a wife could possibly do that.'

'Thank Heaven I am not in that enviable

position !' said Helen, who was still making a desperate effort to steady the corners of her mouth.

Mrs. Vanstone rose with a quiet air of determination. 'I shall go and *listen* to what they are saying,' she said, decidedly. 'When confidence is withheld from me in this outrageous fashion, I am compelled to resort to means which, under happier circumstances, I should be the first to despise;' and with this public palliation of her proceedings she walked off.

'After all, there's a deal of comedy in this life,' thought Helen, as she reflected on recent events. 'I don't expect there's half so much fun to be got in a higher sphere. I think Mr. Weldon has got a touch of humour, and can detect incongruities. I saw a twinkle in his eye once or twice that I rather liked. I declare his visit has quite freshened me up ; it's a long time since I've held intercourse with a man who is gentlemanly and clever too.'

Mrs. Vanstone re-entered the room with a disappointed look.

'They are a cunning pair,' she said, bitterly.

'Your father always mumbles so that nobody can hear him; but that Weldon man has hushed his voice to a whisper. I haven't heard a single word.'

'And yet your ears are pretty acute with long practice, mamma.'

Mrs. Vanstone discreetly allowed this sarcasm to pass without notice, and said,—

'I don't like that young man; there is something very sinister about him.'

'That's because he snapped you up rather sharply once,' said Helen, shrewdly.

'I trust that whatever may be the number of my faults, Helen, paltriness is not to be included among them,' replied her mother, majestically. 'A person can differ from me in argument without making me his enemy. I speak from mature experience. There are symptoms about this man which I could not clearly explain, but which give me the idea of a sinister character.'

'Sinister or not, he has plenty of brains. He is what I call a *man*.'

'I fail to clearly understand what you mean to express by that definition.'

'I mean to say that he is above the average,' answered Helen, rather puzzled to make herself properly understood by a person who had an interest in misunderstanding her. 'He is a man who talks and acts with vigour; is not weak, like papa, for example. He is one whom a woman could look up to with confidence, and suffer herself to be guided by.'

'Don't talk rubbish,' said Mrs. Vanstone, crossly, descending suddenly to homely language. 'In plain English, a man of that sort would develop into a bad-tempered brute a week after marriage.'

'You persistent man-hater! I am sure that Mr. Weldon couldn't be a brute to a woman. In spite of a certain air of sternness about him, he has kind eyes; I know he could be very tender where he loved.'

'For Heaven's sake, Helen, do not distress me with this foolish chatter. I cannot conceive what amusement you derive from speculating about him?'

'My dearest mother, you must remember that the visits of young men to Thomas Street are like angel's visits, and that I am obliged, for lack of occupation, to submit

the character of any new comer to a search-
ing analysis.'

'No eligible young men come this way,'
said Mrs. Vanstone, with her usual bitterness. 'If ever fortune should so far smile
upon us as to permit you to receive an offer
from somebody who could give you a good
home, I should be the first to urge your
acceptance of it ; but I trust, nay I am sure,
that your own good sense will never allow
you to make a fool of yourself by marrying
a man who will bring you to the same
drudging life as this.'

Mrs. Vanstone stole a glance at her
daughter, and saw with inward triumph
that her solemn warning had impressed
her considerably. She was right. Helen
had shrewdness enough to see through a
good many shams, and in consequence of
this faculty, a large proportion of her
mother's proceedings were not sacred in
her eyes ; but she had a very strong belief
in that mother's knowledge both of life and
human nature, and her face wore its gravest
expression as she replied,—

'I know you give me good advice,

mamma. I had better resolve to turn into a regular old maid, with the inevitable cat and parrot, than jump out of the frying-pan into the fire. Here I am poor, but to a certain extent my own mistress. If I married, I should be just as poor, and have to put up with the caprices of a husband into the bargain. For, as you have very wisely hinted, fairy princes don't come down Thomas Street in search of wives, and anybody under a fairy prince I will not accept,' she said, smiling.

Something of her old laughing mood came back to her as she thought more over the subject, for it was in her most amusing manner that she added—

' I have the fate of poor Mrs. Baker next door to warn me against rash matrimony. She was as good-looking when a girl as I am now, I daresay, and you see to what she has descended—eight common-looking children and a dustery kind of arrangement for a house-cap.'

We have seen that Mrs. Vanstone's ears were not acute enough to catch a fragment of the conversation that was being carried

on between the two gentlemen, but being
privileged, we can overhear it from the
beginning.

'I came to your house this evening, Mr.
Vanstone, on the principle that delays are
dangerous,' said Weldon, when the door was
shut on them, and taking care to lower his
voice, in order that if the lady of the house
should be behind the keyhole, as from his
diagnosis of her character he strongly suspected she was, or soon would be, she might
be disappointed.

'No bad news, I hope?' said the other,
turning very pale as he spoke.

'Not exactly, or at least none that need
have a bad result if you act prudently. My
stockbroker told me to-day that they are
going to knock down our shares. I sold
out just before the Exchange closed, and I
strongly advise you to do the same as early
as possible to-morrow morning.'

'They may be down by then,' cried Mr.
Vanstone, anxiously.

'No; the operations will not begin for
another day or two yet, so I am told; but
it is.as well to act soon. The last price,

the one at which I sold, was two and a-half-premium, and you have ten, that will yield you twenty-five pounds less commission ; not so much as we had hoped to get out of them, but still very much better than loss.'

'My dear young friend, I am very much obliged to you for the trouble you have taken,' said the old gentleman, shaking Mr. Weldon's hand with great cordiality. 'Accept my warmest gratitude.'

'You bought them on my recommendation, and I should have blamed myself had you lost. I called here because I happened to be in the neighbourhood, and thought an interview would be better than writing. But I fear it may not have been a very wise step, if you wish, as I suppose you do, to conceal these little transactions from your family,' concluded Mr. Weldon.

The old gentleman coughed, looked embarrassed, and finally made a clean breast of his domestic difficulty. 'Ahem ! I should prefer to keep it quiet, for women are so confoundedly nervous, and always think you are going to lose if you venture into a little bit of speculation. And Mrs. Van-

stone is particularly nervous, as it happens
that I have managed to get rid of a good
part of my income, ha, ha!' and he ended
with a forced laugh, that told Ralph Weldon
plainly enough how very much afraid of
his wife he was.

'I perfectly understand,' replied that
young man of the world drily. To him
it seemed little short of monstrous that a
man should fear a woman.

After a few minutes more had been passed
in conversation upon the subject of the
shares, Mr. Weldon took his leave. As
he passed into the hall, he saw that the
dining-room door was open, and Helen was
seated in such a position that her glance
fell directly upon him.

He had hardly made up his mind whether
he should presume on their brief acquaintance to go in and bid her good-night; but,
in the face of that open door, it would have
been impossible to have avoided the small
courtesy.

Was she secretly desirous of knowing
more of this young man, as he was madly
eager to know more of her? Perhaps so;

for although she had not fallen in love at first sight with him as he unquestionably had with her, he had made a distinct impression upon her fancy; and her voice was full of cordiality as she said,—

'We treat you better than you deserve, you see, Mr. Weldon: you closed your door upon us, we leave ours open to you.'

'It is from your sex that we should especially expect the return of good for evil,' he replied, as his gaze again rested on her with that admiring expression which had caused her to blush so vividly half an hour ago. Even now she could not meet it without a little embarrassment, for she coloured as she answered in a jesting tone.

'That is a very pretty compliment.' She paused as if doubting whether it would be quite correct to give expression to her thought; then added, with the natural audacity that dug so wide a gulf between herself and young ladies who order every word and action according to conventional rules,—'And I should say you are not in the habit of paying compliments.'

It was this audacious frankness which rendered her almost as charming in his eyes as did the radiant beauty which had first stirred his heart.

'You are right, Miss Vanstone, I am not a ladies' man by profession, and for that reason more reliance can be placed upon them.'

Mrs. Vanstone looked up with a displeased air. She was very far from being a prudish mother, but conversation of this kind was hardly such as should have been indulged in between two young persons whose acquaintance was of the very slenderest description.

He caught the glance, readily interpreting its meaning, and willing for his own purposes not to increase the enmity that he had already provoked, held out his hand in token of leave-taking. Yet had the displeasure of a hundred mothers been the consequence, he could not have refrained from detaining that little palm in his own a few seconds longer than was strictly necessary, and he knew by the flush that spread over her cheek, and the droop of the eyes which avoided his last glance, that Helen detected in that swift pressure all that he could have explained.

Mr. Vanstone saw him depart with dismay, for he knew that the shield between himself and a severe domestic storm was now withdrawn. He returned with slow steps to the parlour, and, as he had guessed would be the case, found his wife seated, and waiting for him with that hard look about the eyes, that rigidity about the features, which indicated her firm and unalterable determination to bring the wretched man to book.

' Mr. Vanstone,' began this resolute woman, in her severest tones,—' for more years than I care to remember I have suffered, meekly and resignedly, calamities such as fall to the lot of few women. I have been, sir, a faithful and a true wife, devoted to your interests, careful of your substance, attentive to your wants. I call upon your conscience to answer the question I now put to you—Is this a fitting return for my life of devotion, my ruined hopes, my shattered health ? '

Her manner as she uttered these solemn words was so majestic, that it might have awed a stronger minded man than her husband, and filled him with the uneasy conviction that he had been committing a gross breach of domestic duty.

' My dear, I don't know what you are driving at,' he stammered nervously.

Mrs. Vanstone indulged in a prolonged and withering sneer.

' I am fully acquainted with your deeply-engrained habit of dissimulation, sir; but I will explain my meaning so clearly, that even *you* cannot *shuffle* out of understanding it. I *demand* to know what was your business with that sinister-looking man who thrust himself upon us this night!'

Helen stood by, quietly observant of this small drama, ready to interfere when matters were getting to be too serious. She had assisted at too many of these scenes to be moved by them, and an amused smile curled her lip at her mother's persistent definition of young Weldon as sinister-looking.

Mr. Vanstone was in a most awkward situation. If he told the truth, he knew that his wife's anger would be as great as if he persisted in keeping his own counsel. His occasional speculations on the Stock Exchange had furnished him with nice little sums of money, that enabled him to enjoy himself out to an extent that went some way towards compensating him for his discomforts at home, and he did not relish the idea of either having to renounce the prospect of such an agreeable addition to his modest income, or of having to share it with his family.

' My dear Martha, I don't question you so closely about your proceedings. If a friend of yours happened to call, and be closeted with you for ten minutes, I should not betray curiosity about the matter. Please let us be fair to each other. I don't pry into your affairs ; don't pry into mine. That's just. What do you say, Helen, eh ? '

But before Helen could give an opinion, her mother's wrathful tones rejoined,—

'·How dare you, Mr. Vanstone, institute a comparison between any one of my proceedings and such conduct as that of to-night ? Pry into your affairs, indeed ! If I do *pry*, it

is for your own sake and for the sake of this
poor child here, for the sake of keeping a
roof over our heads, and to prevent you from
squandering your few remaining thousands.'

At this point she reached the melting
stage of her wrath, and burst into tears.

Perhaps the sight of these tears made him
feel less nervous of her than when she fixed
him with her wrathful, glittering glances;
perhaps it was a sudden wave of manly
feeling that for the moment strengthened his
feeble spirit, and prompted him to rebel
against this insidious tyranny.   One thing
is certain, that he resolved to hold his own
this time, and conveyed that resolution in
language that was as emphatic as could be
wished.

'You would like to know what Ralph
Weldon came to see me about, would you,
Mrs. Vanstone?   Well, then, d—n me if I
gratify you!'

And marvelling at his own boldness, the
inspired husband quitted the room, and
hastily getting into bed, pretended to be
asleep when his wife joined him.

Mrs. Vanstone's feelings may be better

imagined than described. Very rarely had it happened to her to be bearded thus; but like all great minds, she accepted her present defeat with calmness, conscious of a future victory that would restore to her her pristine glory.

'I will be at him again to-morrow,' she said to her daughter, as she hastily dried her tears. 'And if he doesn't confess then, I'll keep on till he does. It's evidently something he is ashamed of.'

'If anybody can get out a secret by badgering, it is certainly you, mamma,' answered Helen, laughing. 'Poor papa would have saved himself a deal of trouble by confessing at once. Do you know, I think I shall go to bed now, I feel rather tired.'

And in a few moments she was in her own room, having retired so early, more because she wanted to be alone than because she was really fatigued.

As any judge of human nature might have predicted, her thoughts occupied themselves with this young stranger, whose flattering admiration had been so plainly revealed and she recalled with the faithful memory of one whose uneventful life had made her eager to note trifles, every word, every glance, every gesture that had escaped him during their brief acquaintance.

And then by a transition natural enough, she found herself pondering on the subject of love, of which as yet she knew nothing from her own experience. Was it likely that her own heart should ever be filled with that passionate longing for another— that sweet and strong love of which she had read in books ?—that love which turns the dingiest habitation into an enchanted Eden, and breathes into the life that hitherto appeared so sordid its own radiant glory— the love that turns every work and property of nature into its handmaid and minister.

Would there ever come to her a time in which the small sorrows of her daily life would melt in the great content of a heart that throbbed with new and exquisite emotions; when in the ecstacy of her new-born love, all things would take a fairer hue in her eyes, when sunlit skies, silver waters, the joyous carol of birds, the bloom and fragrance of summer flowers, would seem to speak to her with living voices, as if exulting in her bliss ?

That time was nearer to her than she dreamed of, for all unconsciously had been planted in her heart the tiny seed that was to bring forth golden fruit,—the future had yet in store for her that one supreme and exquisite gift which it bestows but once— the first, passionate love of fresh, unsullied youth.

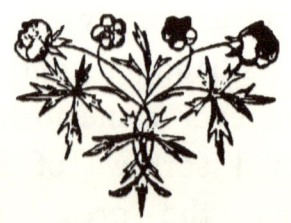

CHAPTER X.

SOWING SEEDS.

T is, or ought to be, always distressing to a high-minded his-
torian to be compelled to recount
an instance of supreme moral
cowardice on the part of those whose actions
he narrates ; and it is, therefore, a painful
task to have to record that the unhappy
Mr. Vanstone was finally vanquished by the
importunities of his wife, and gave, with
great reluctance, a true account of his connection with Ralph Weldon.

But her reception of his intelligence was
very different from what he had expected ;
the upbraiding was of the very mildest description, and a man of less acuteness than
even Mr. Vanstone would have suspected

that the unusual gentleness of her demeanour had its root in some profound and
subtle reasous.   The fact was, that although
bitterly wroth with her husband for not
having allowed his family to share these
windfalls with him, she saw the impropriety
of killing the goose that laid the golden
eggs.   If this young man possessed the
faculty of filling his own pocket, and help-
ing other persons to fill theirs, it was quite
as well that he should be made use of, in
spite of his 'sinister air.'   Mr. Vanstone
had confessed to having netted from his
Stock Exchange proceedings a little over
fifty pounds,—this, as she said to herself
with her profound belief in his deeply-
engrained habits of dissimulation, was most
probably under the mark.   She was perfectly willing that he should continue his
speculations under the prudent directions
of Mr. Weldon, on condition that she took
her portion of the profits.

Such being the workings of her astute
and evenly-balanced mind, it was quite with
her consent that Helen made the following
proposition to her father,—

' Papa, why don't you bring that young Mr. Weldon home one evening ? It would make a change for us, and as he doesn't possess many friends, it might make a change for him too.'

' I can ask him, my dear, if you wish it,' replied her father ; and the result was that two evenings after, Ralph Weldon was seated in the drawing-room of Thomas Street, drinking deeply and greedily from the cup of happiness.

It was an event in the girl's monotonous life, and she had celebrated it with all the resources that lay in her power. She had put on her one grand dress—a blue silk, which fitted her to perfection, and exhibited, to his admiring eyes the faultless symmetry of her tall and supple figure. She had hunted out old bits of lace, and half-forgotten ornaments, and had dressed her smooth, shining hair in the last and most becoming fashion. She smiled to herself as she completed her careful toilet with an air of girlish triumph, for instinct whispered to her that not a detail of it would be lost upon her visitor. ' I wonder whether I really care about his admiration ! I never remember taking such pains before,' she murmured half dreamily.

And when she entered the little drawing-room to greet him, it seemed to Ralph Weldon that she flooded the place with sunshine and perfume. He glanced out on the dull street with its dark, sombre houses, on the mean little apartment with its antiquated, worn-out furniture, and thought what a shame it was that so radiant a creature should be compelled to pass the most glorious days of her youth amid such depressing surroundings. She could not help her poverty, but it would have been possible to have chosen a more congenial spot than this. Nature at least makes no distinction between rich and poor, but showers her gifts ungrudgingly on all, and amid flowers, and light, and fragrant air, and skies undimmed by the smoke of cities, she would have seemed the incarnation of bright and joyous girlhood.

It was doubtless a proof of the attraction of their souls to each other, their marvellous similarity . in thought and nature, that although they were almost perfect strangers so far as actual acquaintance went, they glided into conversatiom with as much freedom from constraint as if they had known each other from childhood. Helen talked as naturally, expressed her thoughts with as little reticence, as if she were addressing her own mother or father, and this young man seemed to understand her perfectly. If she found a momentary difficulty in giving expression to some rather original idea, he supplied the fitting defininition, or the missing word without hesitation. It was as if he could read her very thoughts.

Mrs. Vanstone had not yet put in an appearance, being much busied about the household affairs, and giving last and minute instructions to her inefficient domestic with regard to the serving of the humble banquet; Mr. Vanstone excused himself for a few moments, and thus the young people were left together.

'How do you amuse yourself?' asked Ralph Weldon, rather abruptly.

'I read a good deal. Knowing so few

people as we do, I don't often get a chance of exchanging ideas with my kind, so I hold communion with the mighty dead and the illustrious living,' answered Helen, smiling.

'You don't often go out to parties, picnics, and that kind of thing, I suppose?'

'For often you might say never,' said the girl gravely. 'I think I have been to three parties in my life, and wretched affairs they were. The girls looked nice, and managed to pass muster; but the men were shocking, — they looked so horribly out of place in dress clothes; a cut-away coat and a pipe were more in their way, you know. But I forgot, I did go once to a really splendid ball at my father's cousin's house, Lady Grahame— and there was nothing to offend my susceptibilities there. The women were dressed superbly, and the men had that air which seems to come with wealth and birth; but I didn't enjoy myself really so much as at the humbler gatherings. I liked the glitter of the jewels, the rich sea of colour formed by the dresses, the

music, the brilliant lights ; but I felt too
much out of my element. It was a life I
had dreamed of, but it was not *my* life. I
felt strange and awkward, and seemed at
a loss to know what to say or do. That
was two years ago, I was only seventeen
then ; I think I shouldn't lose my head so
easily now.'

He regarded her with a gaze of infinite
compassion, as he thought how unjust had
fortune been in her instance,—a girl whose
grace and brilliant beauty would have made
her distinguished amid the proudest throng,
condemned to hide her charms in a
wretched hole like this, her greatest
triumph to be the queen of a night in
some assemblage unworthy of her.

'Pardon me for asking so many questions,—but has your father's cousin never
asked you to her other balls ?' he said,
after a pause, in which these and kindred
thoughts had been flitting through his
brain.

'No ; we never got on together. Lady
Grahame presumes upon her rank and
riches to treat papa patronisingly. He

puts up with it, and she thought that I should be as easy. She found out her mistake, and disliked me in consequence. But I don't care a straw for her, or her dislike,' added the girl, with flashing eyes. 'I am her equal in manners, education, and everything else, save insolence, and no being on earth shall patronise me. I would sooner starve than acquire affluence by fawning on a woman of that class.'

'Rich people are only affable to the poor so long as they remain their slaves.'

'I have found out the truth of that in my case, at any rate,' replied Helen, laughing. Somehow there was in her heart to-day so genial a content, such innocent happiness, that she could not look grave even over her social troubles. 'I never go near her ladyship now. Papa keeps up the connection by a monthly visit, and she occasionally condescends to direct her coachman to drive to Thomas Street; but I tell him the relationship is not worth keeping up. After all, even if she were a different sort of woman, pleasant and good-hearted, and took me into society with her, there would be other obstacles. To visit and attend parties a girl must have good dress, and it is impossible that papa could afford it. And I would sooner stop in the house from one year's end to another, than give people the opportunity of sneering at my appearance.'

He could have listened to her for hours, as she poured out to him her girlish confidences; for this talk seemed somehow to bring her closer to him, to make of him, a mere stranger, a sympathetic and sympathising friend.

' Humph, without intending anything impertinent, I think I may conclude that your life is not a very brilliant affair,' he said.

' It is not indeed,' replied the girl, with a grave shake of the head; 'and the worst part is, that there seems no hope of affairs ever getting better.'

' A change might come with marriage,' he suggested, with a rapid glance at her.

She coloured vividly, foolishly, as she said half angrily to herself. ' You speak of an improbability ; it is not at all likely that I shall ever marry.'

He felt his heart sink suddenly at those few quiet words.

' For what reason ? '

' For many reasons,' she answered, in a musing tone. ' In the first place, I should not care to marry a poor man, and it is extremely improbable that any but a poor man would ask me to be his wife ; and, in the second place, I have been so spoiled at home, so accustomed to have my own way, that I should not know how to submit myself with a good grace to the dictation of a man.'

He smiled as he thought that the man who was fortunate enough to win so beautiful a prize, ought only to feel too happy in being *her* slave.

' The majority of men are not tyrants,' he said. ' I think I have seen enough of your household to hazard a pretty shrewd guess that your father is not supreme dictator here, that Mrs. Vanstone is the ruling and guiding spirit.'

' But very few men are so easily ruled

as papa,' replied Helen, with a candour that was not flattering to her absent parent.

Ralph was silent, he could not honestly avow his belief that there were many husbands who would put their necks under the yoke with the meekness of Mr. Vanstone. And it was too early to tell her that he, a man of a totally different mould, would have been ruled by love as completely as the other was ruled by fear, that he would be ready to hug the silken chains which had been bound round him by such dear and tender hands, and that not a shadow should tarnish the lustre of her life save such as the most watchful love could not dispel.

And yet as she sat there in the dim twilight, with her sweet eyes drooped in thought, and the shadows playing over the soft sensitive mouth and the delicate bloom of her fair cheek, an almost irresistible longing came over him to pour out his troubled heart, and tell her of this love, which in so brief a space had attained to a giant's growth. But, with a stern effort, he mastered the fiery impulse, murmuring to himself, 'Not yet, not yet! let

me wait until time has prepared the soil
into which I can plant the flower of ever-
lasting bloom. To force it would be to
kill it.'

Mr. Vanstone came in and lighted the
gas, a task in which Ralph, to show that he
was not troubled with false pride, assisted
him ; and shortly after Mrs. Vanstone sailed
in with her best silk dress, and greeted the
young man, whose sinister air she had for-
merly denounced, with apparent cordiality.
The servant followed quickly, and announced,
in the weak voice of one not accustomed to
such ceremonious proceedings, that the
repast, a kind of tea-dinner, was served ;
and Ralph, politely offering his arm to his
hostess, escorted her down the staircase—a
world too narrow for her noble proportions,
which time had developed freely in spite
of her deep wrongs.

On the whole, it was a merry little party,
for Mrs. Vanstone was gracious, to further
her own purposes. Helen felt strangely
light-hearted and happy ; and Ralph Weldon
developed a fund of humour which hardly
seemed compatible with his usually grave

demeanour. He jested and told comical stories, in a dry, mirth-provoking manner, that made Helen think him the most entertaining person she had ever met. And after the meal was finished, they went back to the drawing-room, and Ralph turned over her music, and stood by her side while she sang.

Then Mrs. Vanstone got him to herself for a few minutes, and after informing him with her sweetest smile that she had discovered her husband's secret, began to sound him on the subject of speculation in connection with the Stock Exchange. And Mr. Weldon, who now perceived the cause of her extraordinary cordiality, saw in what way he could secure her toleration of his visits, and instructed her in all the knowledge he had gained from his friend on the Stock Exchange, in the mysteries of premiums, contangees, and backwardations, and graciously expressed his readiness to help them to add to their small income, by keeping Mr. Vanstone posted with regard to any promising thing in the market, by which he could net ten or twenty pounds profit.

'You must pay me a visit at my little box at Richmond ; my sister will be delighted to make your acquaintance,' he said. 'Next month the country will begin to look at its best. I have a boat, and if you care for the river, I can row you and Miss Vanstone about in the summer evenings.'

'You are very kind, and it would indeed be a pleasure, if my wretched health allowed me to enjoy myself like other people ; but Helen and Mr. Vanstone will, I know, be happy to accept your invitation : she gets so little change, poor child,' replied Mrs. Vanstone, in plaintive tones.

She had developed of late years a slight tendency to rheumatic gout, a malady which was in truth inherited from her ancestors, but which she persisted in attributing to her misfortunes ; although to ordinary minds the connection between rheumatic gout and pecuniary difficulties would be one excessively hard to trace.

'Helen, my love,' she said, raising her voice, 'Mr. Weldon has been kind enough to express a wish that you should visit him at Richmond, and be introduced to his sister.'

'Are you fond of rowing? Because I have a boat,' added Ralph, as she crossed over to where they were sitting.

Her eyes grew bright at the prospect of this simple pleasure.

'O, how delightful! I should like it above all things, Mr. Weldon; and I should be so glad to make the acquaintance of your sister. Is she about my age? I am nineteen, you know.'

'She is twenty-seven, but as merry and light-hearted as a school girl. She is an artist by profession, and will, I hope, one day make a name.'

'I am sure I should take to her, and she to me,' cried Helen, joyously.

He looked at her with a glance, that seemed to say the man or woman who did not take to so charming a girl must be very hard to please.

'And so you live together, like Darby and Joan,' she said, after a pause, in which she had been drawing a mental picture of the Richmond household. 'I suppose that you are very fond of her, and that she worships you.'

'We love each other very dearly; but I am not quite sure that I am altogether such a hero in her eyes as you imagine,' replied Ralph, laughing.

The evening flew on wings, and in an incredibly short time, as it seemed to both himself and Helen, the visitor had to declare that he must take his leave.

'One of the disadvantages of a country life,—having to get up with the sun and quit your friends just as the evening is beginning,' said Helen.

She and her father accompanied him to the street door, while Mrs. Vanstone, in order to maintain the appearance of that cordiality which it was politic to display, smiled benignantly on the group from the top of the staircase, her choice of this safe retreat being dictated by her fear of catching cold.

'Good night! and remember that the moment the fine weather sets in you are to come to Richmond,' cried Ralph, holding out his hand for the second time.

'I shall not forget, but you will see us before then,' said Helen. 'Come in without ceremony any evening you have nothing to do with yourself. You will be sure to find us two lonely females at home. Papa is a wicked man, and generally passes his evenings at the club.'

' May I really be so unceremonious ? ' asked Ralph, with an eager glance.

She coloured ever so little as she answered,—

' I am a straightforward young lady, Mr. Weldon, and mean what I say. If you visit us a few times, you will be able to study my character and find that out for yourself.'

' Then I shall come again very soon,' he said, in a low tone, as he let her hand fall for the last time.

' He improves on acquaintance,' Mrs. Vanstone deigned to admit when they were seated again in the drawing-room.

' He is young in years, but old in thought and experience,' replied the husband, adding, —' He has received a first-rate education, too ; is a better Greek and Latin scholar than ever I was.'

Mrs. Vanstone gave a contemptuous sniff at this remark.

' If he had not learned something better than Latin and Greek, he wouldn't succeed much in the world. Drumming dead languages into your head doesn't give you brains.'

This, of course, was meant for a thrust at her unfortunate lord, on whose mental incapacity she held a very strong opinion.

They still dilated upon the theme of their guest for some time longer, Mrs. Vanstone being very minute in her inquiries as to his antecedents, his mode of life, his probable income, etc., etc. Helen spoke the least of the three ; but in this case silence meant the reverse of indifference.

CHAPTER XI.

ON THE RIVER.

'PAPA! papa! how much longer are you going to be? We shall miss the train to a certainty,' cried the impatient voice of Helen, as she stood in the hall, ready dressed, and waiting for her father to join her.

It was the day of her visit to Ralph Weldon at Richmond, and the girl looked radiant with happiness and the expectation of the pleasures in store for her. Poor child! excursions were rare things with her—especially when undertaken in the society of agreeable young gentlemen,—and this was a day to be marked with white in her calendar. Mrs. Vanstone, who detested even the shortest railway journey, and would have screamed with horror at the thought of jeopardising her precious person in a rowing boat, had declined to make one of the party, on the convenient plea of failing health. To her infinite credit it must be stated, that she had pinched out of their small means a sum sufficient to buy Helen a very pretty costume, in order that she might not suffer from juxtaposition with Miss Weldon. Every person has some good points, and Mrs. Vanstone's lay on the side of her maternal instincts.

It was the first week in June; the greater part of May had been cold and cheerless, but at last summer had come in with a sudden rush, and flooded the earth with green, and perfume, and sunshine. Even dingy Thomas Street seemed a little lighted up with the prevailing gladness, and exhibited its sympathy with nature by putting forth a flower or two in its desolate gardens.

Mr. Weldon was at the station to receive them, habited, as became a dweller amid rural delights, in a light suit and a straw hat.

' How nice and cool you look, while poor

papa seems as hot and uncomfortable as can well be in that black coat and heavy hat,' cried Helen, laughingly, as she shook hands with him. Smiles overflowed her mouth constantly to-day, for her heart was full of a girlish gladness and content.

'I hope you will have so fallen in love with the country before you return, Miss Vanstone, that I shall be able to persuade you to become my near neighbour,' said Ralph, as he assisted her into a fly.

At the end of a quarter of an hour, they drew up before a small house, half villa, half cottage, the lower windows of which were screened from observation by a thick high hedge that divided the garden from the road. A neat maid-servant came to open the gate, and as they walked up the pavement leading to the door, Helen caught a side glimpse of a spacious, well-kept lawn, bordered by rose-trees. Some delicious-looking roses bloomed close to the windows, and filled the warm air with a fragrant perfume.

'O, what a delightful place this is!' cried Helen, stopping short in her ecstasy, and bending down to inhale the delicious scent from the roses. The gay tints and perfume of the flowers, the pure, cool green of the grass, the golden flood of sunshine, the joyous carol of the birds as they clustered among the branches, filled her heart with their own unconscious joy. For the language of nature had been almost a sealed book to this young dweller in cities. And Ralph's dark cheek flushed with pleasure as he noted her simple delight; and he said kindly,—

' I must make up a basket of these roses for you to take home,'

' Oh, thank you very much, but it would be robbing your beautiful garden.'

' I would strip it of every flower it holds to keep that look of delight on your face,' he said earnestly.

She did not blush at that meaning tone, but she returned his gaze with one that was half shy, and half grateful, and wholly expressed her consciousness of what was passing in his thoughts as he spoke thus.

' I will go in now and see your sister; there will be plenty of time to make a further acquaintance with the flowers,' she said a little shyly.

Ralph led them into the hall, and Miss Weldon, hearing them enter, came out to meet them. She was a pleasant looking girl, rather below the middle height, but graceful and lady-like in her movements. She had her brother's dark eyes and hair, but here their resemblance to each other ceased, for while Ralph's expression was one of gravity, not unmixed with sternness, her features wore a constant smile, and her clear joyous tones indicated a sunny nature.

The two girls went up-stairs for a few moments, and Clara Weldon began to chatter to her guest without loss of time.

'Miss Vanstone, I am so very pleased to know you; my brother has sung your praises to me from the first night he saw you. I fully expected to see you last month, but my tiresome illness intervened, although, as it happens, you could not have had nicer weather for your first visit. Ralph described you to me very minutely, you know. I used to tell him I was sure I could paint your portrait from his description.'

'Indeed!' cried poor Helen, blushing a little under the gaze of those eyes which were so marvellously like Ralph's. 'And I have heard a great deal about you, too—I so long to see your pictures.'

'O, you will not behold anything very elaborate, I assure you. I am only one of the "small fry" yet, and think myself a genius if I make over two hundred a-year.'

'Two hundred a year!' cried Helen, opening her eyes in astonishment. 'Why, that is a fortune for a girl to make, I mean by her own exertions. I only wish I possessed a talent that would bring me in a fourth of that.'

The slight flush of excitement that dyed her cheek, as she spoke with an energy called forth by the subject, made her look lovely, and Clara Weldon's gaze dwelt on the sweet face with the admiring gaze of an artist.

'My brother told me you were very beautiful, and he was quite right. Forgive my impertinent compliment, my dear; but I am a lover of beauty by profession.'

Apparently the young ladies had been closeted together too long to please Mr. Ralph Weldon, for his impatient voice called out from the foot of the little stairs,—

'We are getting very tired of waiting here.'

'That means he wants you, Miss Vanstone,' said Clara Weldon, laughing.

When they went down, he proceeded to explain his programme to his guests.

'It is now half-past four. We will have what Clara intends to give us to fortify ourselves as soon as possible. After that we will devote a quarter of an hour to the inspection of the botanical arrangements. A fly will then be here to take us to the river, and we will row about till dusk, return back in time for a hasty supper, and put you safely in the last train for town. Will this suit you, Miss Vanstone?'

'Splendidly! I think you are a first-rate organiser, Mr. Weldon.'

'I am glad it meets with your approval. Clara, is the banquet spread?'

And on receiving an answer in the affirmative, they proceeded into the dining-room, where they were regaled with a choice little dinner of salmon, lamb, and other dishes, and vegetables, the product of their own kitchen garden.

Everything about this small home was characterised by an elegance and refinement which charmed Helen, accustomed to one so totally different. The order, the cleanliness, the pretty though inexpensive knick-knacks arranged tastefully about the rooms, bore witness to the care of a mistress who took pride in her house, and was enabled to create an agreeable and pleasing effect out of humble material. Even the linen which adorned the table seemed to look whiter than that on which they took their meals in Thomas Street.

' But I daresay their income is more than treble our own. What can be done on two hundred and fifty a-year,' thought the girl to herself, as her glance took in all these details with something like a feeling of envy. She did not know that a discontented mistress makes a gloomy home, whatever the means she may have at her command. Order and neatness would always have flourished where

Clara Weldon was the presiding genius, for she infused her own qualities into everything around her.

They had not much time for an inspection of the garden, for the fly was waiting at the gate when they left the dinner table, and Ralph Weldon took them very quickly over the small estate.

'For you know that the river is the great feature of our entertainment,' he said to them.

So they got into the fly, and were deposited at the boathouse, where the stylish appearance of the two girls and the beauty of one attracted the regards of several young men in acquatic costumes lounging about.

'It is a remarkable trait of the average Briton, that while he can hardly open his mouth before a woman to whom he is introduced for the first time, he can always stare at her by the hour together,' remarked Ralph, with a displeased air, as he put off from the shore with a few vigorous strokes. And Helen, who divined by whom that remark had been called forth, showed her consciousness by one of those glances in which shyness and pleasure met, and which gave to her eyes one of their sweetest expressions.

Mr. Vanstone established himself comfortably on the cushions, and lighted a cigar at the express command of his hostess, who assured him emphatically that smoking was not in the least disagreeable to her; while Helen assumed the command of the steering arrangements, being appointed to this office by Ralph, in spite of her laughing protest that she had never steered before in her life.

' I shall run you ashore in no time, I know.'

' Oh no, you will not; I will tell you which string to pull,' replied Ralph, who enjoyed her pretty puzzled looks, like an infatuated young man as he was; for her sweet presence made this ordinary little boat more splendid in his eyes than Cleopatra's famous barge.

' How do you like rural life?' he asked, as he rested on his oars.

' So much, that I am very sad at the prospect of having to return to London. I should like to live here for a month.'

' That can very easily be managed. Come down as soon as you like, and stay till you are tired. I promise you will not outwear your welcome.'

'Oh, Mr. Weldon, I was not fishing for an invitation,' cried she.

'I never suspected you were. You are not one of the fishing sort; but I am fishing to get you down amongst us.' And as she drooped her eyes beneath his earnest glance, he went on eagerly,—'I would row you about as long as you liked. Will you come?'

'I cannot make a promise just now. I should like it above all things; but I must consult mamma about it,' she answered shyly.

'I should have thought you were a young lady who was rather independent of mamma,' he said, plunging his oars sharply into the water.

'You do not think I am rude; you are not offended with me, I hope?'

'Not offended, but—very disappointed, that is all,' he replied.

'I will *try* to come; I don't think I can promise more.'

'And that means we shall have you,' he said with a radiant look.

So he rowed on in silence, thinking what a paradise that little home would be if it were lightened with her bright smile and sunny glances. The world had changed to him during those few weeks in which he had dared to indulge in the hope that he might win this young girl's love. His heart took a quicker beat from the beauty round him, and his eyes dwelt with a keen interest on things that he had never cared to notice hitherto. For the thought of her wove itself into everything on which his glance fell and his touch lighted. The magic lights and tints which nature scatters in profusion on her countless creations— the silver sparkle of the shifting waters, the golden glories of the summer sunset, the rich bloom of the summer flowers, became to him things of greater beauty since he had known her; for all that was sweet, and tender, and fragrant in these, seemed mingled in her smile, and glance, and hair.

The soft, rosy twilight fell about them, bathing the fair face in its tender shadows as they floated on in the sweet silence, and the tranquil beauty of the scene, the balmy odours of the delicious night, seemed to enter into his soul and blood, and open his heart wider and wider to its passionate love.

CHAPTER XII.

FIRST LOVE.

'YOUR roses!' cried Ralph, suddenly remembering his promise, as they stood in the drawing-room, looking at Clara Weldon's last picture.

'How good of you to think of them; but have we time?' asked Helen.

'You need not start for a quarter of an hour yet. Will you take this little basket and come into the garden with me, and I will gather them for you?'

'Can I help you?' asked Mr. Vanstone, who had been favoured with private instructions from his wife not to leave these young people alone more than could possibly be helped, and was making a feeble effort to do his duty.

'We will not trouble you ; it hardly re-
quires three persons for such little work,'
replied Ralph quickly. 'One to hold the
basket, and one to cut are quite enough.
Are you ready, Miss Vanstone, because we
have not too much time ?'

She took up the basket, with cheeks that
were just a little brighter than their wont,
and followed him into the garden. There
were a few precious moments left, and he
intended to make the most of them. The
presence of these other people had been a
disagreeable restraint upon him all day, but
now he would have her to himself for one
delicious little interval, and be able to feast
his gaze on her delicate beauty without the
fear of being watched.

The sky was cloudless, and had hung out
its starry jewels long ago, while the soft
breeze, laden with the fragrant odours of
the balmy, summer night, fanned her cheek
and brow. Glorious as had looked the
fair face of nature, when lighted up a few
hours since with that golden flood of sunshine, it seemed to Helen that it looked
fairer still under the silver light and the

quivering shadows which night had woven for its veil.

They began their task, and the roses were placed one by one in the basket. In this agreeable occupation they were necessarily brought very close together, so close that he could feel her fragrant breath upon his cheek, so close that once the sweet, sensitive mouth, with its full coral lips, was within an inch of his own.

He had taken the basket from her hands in order to adjust the flowers a little more neatly, while she watched him with glad, laughing eyes. Then all at once he let the basket fall to the ground, and taking the astonished girl's hands into his own, spoke with the fiery vehemence born of great passion.

'Helen, could you not bear to live here always? I love you, my darling, tenderly, passionately, as a man never loves but once. From the first hour I saw you, you filled my heart with glory and sunshine, and I cannot dare to think of life without you. Can you love me a little in return?'

She neither stirred nor spoke, but her

lips parted into a smile that was almost in-
fantine in its joy, and into the sweet, dark
eyes there came such a light as could have
been kindled by the words of none save
him. In her eyes and on her lips he read
his answer, and drew her to his breast.

'And you love me?' he whispered, as
his hand strayed fondly over the shining
hair.

'I do,' she answered, with the frankness
of one whose soul was filled too full of joy
to hide or to coquet with her feelings.

'And you, my darling, have made the
world look so bright to me,' he said. 'Once
I was foolish enough to harbour the notion
that a mysterious fate had debarred me from
the delights that others extract from life. I
fancied that my heart would never throb
with those exquisite emotions, that deep
and passionate love, which turns earth into
an Eden. For there have been things in
my history, Helen,—I shall tell you all some
day, for no secrets shall be kept from my
darling,—which have weighed upon my spirit,
and darkened it with heavy shadows. But
it is all over now,' he added, in joyous, ring-

ing tones,—' the shadows are lifted, the past is forgotten, and I live in the glorious sunshine of the present, in the consciousness of having won for myself a priceless jewel—the rich, unfailing treasure of your love.'

He stooped down and kissed the soft, sweet mouth, that mouth from which had come the little word which had made him feel rich above all living men ; that mouth from which, had she so chosen it, there could have issued words that could have stung and festered in his heart like poisoned arrows.

'And my own sweet Helen, we will create for ourselves such happiness as only poets have dreamed of.   We have youth and health, and we will make life one complete holiday. And although I am not poor now, in a year or two I shall be much richer,—I will tell you all about my prospects in time—and then I shall be able to give you all that you desire, splendid jewels, rich dresses, a carriage, a beautiful home !'

And Helen listened trustingly to this sanguine talk.   What lovers ever yet pictured the future without the most radiant of skies, the most resplendent of suns ?

Love hushes reason to sleep with a few witching words, and speaking to them with the language of hope, persuades them that it is the language of reality.

'The world has changed to me too,' she said, shyly, as she nestled her head against the strong shelter of that breast. 'Before I knew you I was discontented, and soured, and miserable, hating and despising the sordid life which had been assigned me by the fault of others; but *now*—I cannot explain all I feel, Ralph, it would want a poet to do that,—but I am *so changed*. The old discontented Helen has vanished, and in her stead I find a girl whose heart seems to have woke from a long, long sleep, and to throb with a strong and passionate life!'

And thus, amid the breathless silence of the summer night, did these two lovers pour out to each other their sweet and tender secrets, attaining in those few supreme moments the height of human bliss . . . And ever in their after lives rearing itself high, and towering against all weaker and less exquisite recollections, did there stand out the one imperishable memory of that one brief hour, when the hand of love struck to a divine music the chords of her spirit, and their souls seemed to melt into each other and become one with the first passionate kiss that was laid upon her lips.

. . . 'My roses!' she said, stooping down to put them back into the basket.

'My darling, they are blooming in our hearts!'

CHAPTER XIII.

A RELUCTANT CONSENT.

'MY dear child, to put it in plain English, there will be the deuce to pay when your mother hears of this,' said Mr. Vanstone, when his daughter had confided to him her secret, amid the jolting and rumbling of the train.

The girl turned a shade paler at the prospect of her mother's hostility to her wishes. 'But, papa dear, you will stand by me, will you not?'

'I will do all I can, my love; but you know I have found it a tough job to fight my own battles for the last twenty years,' replied the father, with a comical expression of countenance; for Mr. Vanstone was not without a touch of humour, and was not at all averse to occasionally indulge in a smile at his own expense,—an enviable faculty, which enables a man to support the trials of life with greater cheerfulness than those who possess it not.

'Of course, I know mamma will think I ought to marry somebody in a better position,' continued Helen, gravely; 'but to bother about position is simply nonsense. We have grand relations, it is true, but they wouldn't stir their little fingers to find me a husband; and, after all, papa, they never did anything for us yet, and never will. The world with which I come into contact does not think a bit better of Miss Helen Vanstone because she has got a wealthy uncle, and a cousin a Baronet's wife. People have a habit of taking you for what you are, not what you were.'

'That is undeniably true,' assented Mr. Vanstone,—who had discovered that fact long before his daughter was born.

'I will never give him up to please anybody. If mamma holds out, I will go out one fine morning and marry him privately,' she added, with an air of determination.

If Mr. Vanstone had been a judicious parent, he would have undoubtedly remonstrated with his child on the heinousness of such unfilial sentiments, but he was also a much-suffering husband, and to know or see that his wife was being thwarted was one of the small delights of his life, and the only compensation which fate seemed to allow him for his own private wrongs.

'You have no objection to my marrying him, have you, papa?' she asked.

'My dear, I think it would be a very good match for you, under the circumstances. Ralph Weldon is a clever young fellow, and will make his way in life.'

'Then, it is all right!' cried Helen, radiantly. 'You are the head of the family, not mamma, and if you give your consent, I need have no scruple.'

Flattering as was this declaration to a man's vanity, it must be owned that Mr. Vanstone had the good sense to receive it with a few grains of salt.

'I am the nominal head, I know, dear

but your mother is a woman of very strong will, and she has acquired a confirmed habit of having her own way.'

' But she cannot have it in this instance, papa. You and I and Ralph, all leagued together, will surely be more than a match for her.'

Mr. Vanstone shook his head dubiously. ' I am not so sure of that, Helen.'

Bnt love gives great courage to even the faintest heart as well as to one naturally resolute, and when she entered the dingy precincts, which seemed more odious than ever in comparison with that dear little home she had just quitted, she felt herself capable of fighting a harder battle than this.

Mrs. Vanstone was not, as it happened, in the sweetest of moods, for although she had declined to accompany them, her loneliness had made her feel cross and spiteful. Helen began by flourishing the basket of flowers in her face.

' Here are beautiful roses that Mr. Weldon has sent to you, mamma.'

This was not quite the truth, as we know ;

but she thought that the harmless little false-hood, combined with their bloom and fra-grance, might have a benignant influence.

'Pity to cut them ; they will soon wither here,' was the ungracious response.

It was very evident that Mrs. Vanstone was not amenable to delicate flattery that evening. A less determined girl might have preferred to wait for a more favourable opportunity, but her love made her restless and impatient. She was resolved to have this matter settled one way or the other before she went to rest.

'Mamma, I have something of great importance to communicate to you,' she said, plunging *in medias res.* 'Ralph Weldon has proposed to me, and I have promised to marry him.'

Had a bomb-shell suddenly exploded in the room, her mother could not have worn a more startled expression. As might have been expected from a lady of . her peculiar temperament, her wrath first directed itself against her husband.

'How came it that you left these silly creatures together, after receiving my expressed injunctions to the contrary, Mr. Vanstone ?' she asked, severely.

'I could not watch them like a little dog,' he replied, with some spirit.

'A little dog would have proved himself a much more efficient protector,' retorted his better half, with withering scorn.

'Come, mamma, it is hardly fair to vent your temper upon him,' struck in Helen. 'Vent it upon me, if you like ; I am the guilty person.'

'There is no guilt at all in the matter,' cried Mr. Vanstone, buttoning up his coat with the air of a man who is determined to exercise his authority for once. 'This young fellow loves her very dearly ; and I say that, under the circumstances, it is as good a match as she can expect. Ralph Weldon has got his head screwed on the right way, and is a man who will make money.'

'So, that is your opinion,' said his wife, sarcastically. 'Thank heaven, my child has yet *one* parent left capable of attending to her interests.'

'Of course I shall institute inquiries into

his means, his prospects, and all that kind of thing,' added Mr. Vanstone, with a last expiring effort.

'You need not trouble yourself, *I* shall attend to these matters.'

Finding that his overtures were so unfavourably received, Mr. Vanstone undid the buttons of his coat, surrendering by this significant action the authority which he had for a moment assumed, plunged his hands into the pockets of his trousers, and retired into the privacy of his own thoughts. There are moments when silence becomes the wisest and most dignified policy, and he was assured in his own mind that the present was one of them.

Mrs. Vanstone chewed the bitter cud of her reflections. She did not know on what grounds to openly condemn, and yet she could not bring herself to heartily approve this engagement. The truth was, she had still in her secret soul dared to harbour ambitious hopes of Helen's future, to cherish the fond notion that her beauty would, in spite of their misfortunes, succeed in attracting some eligible suitor, who would raise them into a better position. Where this generous wooer was to come from, or by what combination of favouring circumstance, he would be led into the unfamiliar regions of Thomas Street, she had never been successful in indicating clearly to herself. But like all people who cherish delusive and impracticable notions, she had clung to her belief all the more firmly, because she was unable to base it upon any solid or enduring data.

As a dead silence had reigned since Mrs. Vanstone's snappish answer effectually quenched her husband's unwonted audacity, and reduced him to that passive condition which was his normal one in her presence, Helen thought that it was a fitting opportunity for her to speak.

'You know, mamma, I have often told you that I had made up my mind to live and die an old maid, and up to within a few weeks, my experience of the very few men with whom we have come into contact, had not inspired me with any desire for a different destiny. But since I have known Ralph Weldon, my heart has opened itself to the longings natural, I suppose, to my sex and my age, and I have felt a better and a happier girl for the change.'

She paused a moment, and when she resumed, the simple pathos in her voice, the soft flush on her cheeks, the tender light in the sweet dark eyes, bore such direct witness to the joy with which this new-born love had filled her whole soul, that even Mrs. Vanstone was softened, and was carried away to the far-off years when she, too, had shared the delusions of girlhood, and dreamed of such happiness as her child was dreaming of now.

'I don't suppose it is natural for any woman to go through life with her mission in the world unfulfilled, and to find herself standing solitary and desolate on the shores of time, while the sullen tide rolls backwards and forwards without laying at her feet a single precious gift. I thought it might be easier to me than most, from the conditions of my present existence; and so, but for Ralph's advent, it might have been. He has taught me a different creed, and his love has infused into the future a light that makes it look hopeful and golden. I love him, and I shall only know happiness by becoming his wife.'

As she ended, the tears fell, in spite of her brave attempt to hold them back, and perhaps it was the sight of them that pleaded her cause most effectually with her mother, whose own eyes were moist when she replied,—

'Your happiness is as dear to me, Helen, as to yourself, and if I appeared to thwart your wishes, it was because experience has taught me to look for the shadows where youth only sees sunshine. If your heart is set upon marrying this young man, and he can show me that he possesses the means to give you a home which, if not such as I could wish for you, will be one a little better than that you have had hitherto, I will not say nay. My duty, my love for you, will not let me rest content with anything short of a rigid examination into all these, what may seem to you trifling details.'

Helen crossed to her mother's side, and flung her arms round her neck.

'Oh no, dearest mother, you are quite

right. I know it is your love that makes you so anxious, and you must forgive me if I have seemed unkind and impetuous. But if you could guess how very dear he is to me!'

Mr. Vanstone, finding that his wife's feelings were considerably softened, considered that he might, with safety, hazard a remark of a general nature.

'It carries one back to the days of one's own youth, eh, Martha?'

Mrs. Vanstone shook her head, not exactly in a cross fashion, but with an air that seemed to indicate she had no desire to be taken back to them.

'If their youth doesn't open with brighter promises than ours, Gabriel, it will be but a poor look-out for them,' she said, chillingly.

'It seems that I can never say or do anything right,' muttered poor Mr. Vanstone, as he re-thrust his hands into his pockets, and retired for the second and last time into himself.

So the battle was won; and before she went to bed that night, Helen penned a hasty note to her lover, according to promise, to let him know the attitude of her mother; for he was to call to-morrow evening and make a formal demand for her hand.

She had a little difficulty with regard to the manner in which she should address him : should it be 'Dear Ralph,' or 'Dearest Ralph.'

'Oh, how absurd it is playing the coquette with the man I love, and whom I am going to marry,' she cried, when she had pondered over the subject for a few seconds. So the letter went with the more affectionate prefix.

'My Dearest Ralph,—Mamma is quite prepared to give her consent, and papa gave his as we came along in the train, so there are no difficulties in the way. I shall expect you to-morrow. I cannot write any more, for I am now very tired and sleepy. With best love, I remain, your affectionate and happy   Helen.'

He found his first love-letter waiting for him in the morning; and Ralph Weldon, grave, staid young man as he was, did what a schoolboy would have done, pressed it to his lips.

He came the next evening, and received from her parents the formal consent to their engagement. He gáve Mrs. Vanstone all the information she required with regard to his income and prospects, and consented, though with some reluctance, to her request that at least a year should elapse before Helen left her home.

'I am very averse to hasty marriages,' she explained. 'Half of the unhappiness of married life arises from the tendency which seems common to all young lovers to enter at once into this solemn contract without sufficient experience of each other's temperament, tastes, and habits. Helen is still very young, only nineteen, and you know positively nothing of her character, as she knows nothing of yours. A year is a short enough period in which to cultivate that necessary knowledge. I do not wish to damp you, but it may happen that in that time you may discover in her, or she in you, certain qualities and inclinations which might prove fatal to your married happiness.   If such exist, which I trust they do not, it is better for both that they should be discovered before than after.'

There was so much common sense in these reasons, that Ralph hardly knew with what arguments to oppose them, so he yielded with a protest.

'A year does certainly not make much difference in a lifetime, but when a man loves as deeply as I do, he likes to make sure of his prize, and I shall always feel a little uneasy until Helen is made mine, beyond the power of man or fate to take her from me.'

'I think you may trust in the stedfastness of her affection,' replied the mother; adding, with a quiet smile, 'and if she changes in a year, she would have made but a discontented wife.'

On the whole, Ralph was very glad when that interview terminated, for Mrs. Vanstone's prudent reasons and unpleasant manner of summing up contingencies, seemed to drive some of the sunshine out of his heart, and fill it with cold, prophetic shadows.

'My darling, you must come down and

stay with Clara as soon as possible,' he said to Helen in the course of that evening. 'Our love seems out of harmony with this gloomy place. You must come among the sunshine and the flowers—our hearts will breathe more freely then!'

CHAPTER XIV.

HALCYON DAYS.

WHEN the time came for Helen to fulfil her promise of spending a week at Richmond with her lover, she had a fit of contrition, in which she accused herself for being an ungrateful wretch to leave her mother for the society of any young man, however lovable and charming. Since, with this sensitive young soul, to feel and to speak were one, she lost no time in revealing to Mrs. Vanstone her deep sense of her filial ingratitude. The worthy woman received the confession with that nicely-balanced demeanour which impresses a sensitive culprit more strongly than the keenest reproaches. A reproach provokes a reaction, and leads you to defend yourself;

but when a person looks profoundly miserable, sighs deeply, and says nothing, the eloquence of such silence is terrible.

Mrs. Vanstone did three things,—she heaved a profound sigh, she then smiled a little bitter smile, in which there was no mirth, and finally closed her eyes with the air of one who was shutting them from a painful vision. Helen well knew that these three single acts were with her mother signs of the deepest tribulation, and felt herself driven to despair. It was not unlikely that, in the fervour of her penitence, she would have exhorted Mrs. Vanstone to write a letter then and there, bidding Ralph Weldon go his ways and never more to disturb the even tenour of their lives, but there was something stronger even than the love for a mother which kept her from offering this painful sacrifice. She was looking on a vision of her own, a roseate one; she was thinking what a Paradise that little river-side home would be when Ralph walked by her side, and told her all manner of things sweet for maidens to hear, in those tender thrilling tones of his.

' Oh, why did I ever fall in love ; why did
I ever get engaged ?' she cried, with an
almost comical petulance.

This was too good an opportunity to let
slip. If there was one method of attacking
her opponents dearer to Mrs. Vanstone than
another, it was that which is known as the
oblique.

' Because it is the pleasure of all foolish
and headstrong girls to despise the admoni-
tions of their elders and superiors, to court
the misfortune that they ought to shun.'

' Oh, mamma dearest, please do not talk so
terribly ; it chills me;' cried poor Helen, en-
treatingly. ' I cannot think of Ralph, and
associate him with unkindness, neglect, and
indifference. If you could only see how
different he is from other men,—how tender,
how considerate ! '

Mrs. Vanstone laughed the hollow laugh
of the worldly-wise and cynical at this
entreaty. She rose from her seat with the
air of a Siddons. Decidedly this woman
would have made her fortune on the stage.

' Go, poor, foolish girl ; go to your doom !
I would have saved you had it been possible.'

Helen's obstinacy rendering the hope of salvation impossible, the result was that she set out for Richmond, after taking a most heartrending farewell of her mother, and shedding many salt tears. Even at the last, as she was about to descend the stairs with tottering steps, she called out, in earnest tones,—

' Tell me to stay now, and I will.'

To this offer Mrs. Vanstone, her handkerchief to her eyes, replied in a firm voice, indicative of her resolution to suffer, and even die, rather than prove herself a selfish mother,—

' No, I can bear it.'

Helen and Mr. Vanstone got into the cab, and after they had gone a little way, she said to him through her tears,—

' Papa, I find it is a terrible thing to be engaged.'

The poor gentleman heaved a deep sigh.

' That is not the worst part of the business, my dear. Marriage is the most terrible part.'

The earnest, hearty manner in which he pronounced these few words, was so intensely comic, when taken in conjunction with his own experiences, that Helen smiled in spite of her woes.

'You dear, old, philosophical papa,' she said, kissing him : ' but, you know, you have been a very naughty man to us.'

At the Richmond station, Ralph was there to receive them ; and as there was a crowd on the platform, their meeting was in no way lover-like, but tranquil and dignified. Yet the hearts of both were beating quickly, and any intelligent observer could have read the state of the case, both in his fervent glances and the lovely flush which settled on her fair cheek. In the silent rapture of that meeting even Mrs. Vanstone was forgotten for a moment.

They reached the cottage, and were welcomed heartily by Clara Weldon. Being a discreet and kind-hearted young lady, she thought it was high time the lovers had a few moments alone, and cleverly drew off Vanstone *père* under pretence of showing him the garden.

Then, when they were alone, Ralph drew her to him, and kissed her so much and so fervently, that at length she recoiled from him, half scared and half offended.

'I did not think you were going to receive me like that,' she said, with her face the colour of a rose.

'Is it a way that offends you, dearest? he asked.

'No, not quite that,' she answered hastily. She saw the slight cloud that came over his brow, and divined the cause. 'But—but you are a little boisterous. We have only been engaged a few days, and I have always heard that a lover should ask and not take. A young lady who does not value her own self-respect may end by perceiving that others do not value it also.'

She said all this with the most enchantingly severe air of youthful wisdom in the world; and all the while that she was preaching prudery so admirably, the smiling mouth, the tender eyes, contradicted her words, and told that she loved him as dearly as he loved her. And he adored her all the more for this charming, unaffected modesty, which proved her no worldly-experienced coquette, no young forward flirt, who had been polluted with the kisses of half-a-dozen lovers before. The language of love was as new to her as to him. Thank heaven! in these days it was something for a man to be grateful for to know that he was the first.

'You are an angel of purity and goodness, you dear little preacher, and I am an uncouth, savage Bohemian. Henceforth I will never take a kiss without your permission. Is that conduct sufficiently respectful?' She smiled, and said it was.

After a while she spoke as follows,—

'You must know, Ralph, it is very likely I shall be dull and mopish for a day or two, because I shall be thinking of poor mamma sitting by herself in that dreary, dismal house.'

In his heart Ralph Weldon was of opinion that his future mother-in-law was a selfish, peevish woman, who extracted positive delight out of her woes; but he played the hypocrite well enough to express regret for her condition. Still there was a want of sincerity in his tones which Helen detected at once, for she rejoined,—

'But if you love me, I must insist upon your loving my mamma, sir. She is the dearest, kindest, sweetest of mothers; and if she received you a little coldly at first, you must remember it is you who have offended by coming to steal her darling away. Oh yes, sir, I know what you are going to say, that it was not your fault; but she thinks it was, and I think so too. Why did you not keep away from our house?'

'How could a man refuse to enter Paradise when opened to him?'

'How very grandiloquent you artists are, to be sure, and what nonsense it is.' Then she added directly, with true feminine inconsistency, 'but I think I prefer it to sense, on the whole. But to return to our subject; you will love mamma for my sake, will you not?'

'I will try my best, dearest,' said Ralph, gravely.

'I know that to strangers she must appear a little cold and hard; but then consider how she has been tried—all her youthful hopes and illusions dissipated in a moment by papa's folly.'

'From what little I have seen of your household,' said Ralph, quietly, 'I fancied that Mr. Vanstone hadn't an easy time of it.'

Helen coloured faintly under her lover's penetrating eye. 'Of course, mamma has never forgiven him for it, and sometimes she upbraids him a little more bitterly than —well, than I would, were I in her place.'

'I don't think you resemble your mother to any great extent, dear,' answered Ralph, with a peculiar smile. 'I cannot fancy you making my life bitter to me for any injury of that nature.'

At that direct appeal, enthusiasm came out and conventionality went in.

'Oh, my darling, I should always love you the same, however unfortunate you were,' she said fervently, and with a little guilty thrill of pleasure at the epithet she bestowed on him for the first time.

'You sweet enthusiast,' he said, regarding her tenderly, 'one thing I am sure of,—if you love me as well as you love your mother, I shall be the happiest husband in England.'

' The love is so different, Ralph,' she murmured softly, as she lifted her pure, truthful
eyes half timidly to his own.

Then, just as they had arrived at a most
satisfactory state of mutual tenderness and
content, Mr. Vanstone made his appearance,
with that want of propriety which is characteristic of elderly and prosaic people. The
intrusion of a third party at such a moment
is superlatively chilling ; they came down at
a leap from the rosy Paradise inhabited by
lovers to this work-a-day world, in which
people babble of the weather, politics, of
every topic, in fact, that has no interest for
young souls enamoured of each other.

But after a day or two, thanks to the
management and tact of Clara Weldon, who
was in her way a subtle diplomatist, the life
at the cottage was fixed in certain grooves.
The old gentleman was cleverly got out of
the way, and made infinitely happy, by the
constant supply of excellent cigars. In fine,
he enjoyed himself so thoroughly ; it was
so refreshing to feel himself treated courteously, and to be safe from the irruption of
a splenetic spouse, that he felt quite sad at

the prospect of ever leaving so delightful a spot.

And how did the lovers spend their days? Why, like most other young persons in their condition. They spent the greater portion of their time in Ralph's painting-room,—he working away at his picture, she watching him. They babbled together much, of course, for they had all their past to unfold to each other, all their secret thoughts, dreams, and aspirations to communicate, until their inmost souls were fairly exchanged. What they said in those moments, tedious enough to a third person, but full of exquisite joy to them, may be better imagined than described. The talk of lovers, like the talk of children, sounds dull when put on paper,—for it is the kindling eye, the glowing cheek, the eloquent voice which give the charm to their words, and make poor stuff sound like the communing of angels. The three simple words, ' I love you,' do not look much written, but when they are uttered by a beautiful young creature, pure and fresh as the dew and the morning, in a voice of sweetest music, they

stir the pulse and thrill the heart with a
power one must feel to believe.

And then, when they were tired of
babbling their sweet nonsense to each other,
there came an interval of delicious silence, of
that dreamy contemplation beloved of young
and amorous hearts, when sweeter visions are
conjured up than the most eloquent lips
could pourtray. She was the happiest of
women, for every moment revealed the
ardent love, the chivalrous tenderness of her
betrothed; and he was the happiest of men,
since every hour strengthened the claims of
this beautiful young creature on his heart
and faith. He knew that what charmed him
most in her was the exquisite blending of
love and dignity: it was a temperament
southern in its intensity and capacity for
passion, overlaid and held in check by a
northern training. How he loved to see
the combat between nature and convention,
and how his heart thrilled when the impetuous words that expressed her soul rushed to
her lips in spite of an almost ludicrous effort
to keep them back. From this cause there
arose inconsistencies that were charming,

that gave to their love-making a character of its own.   Once she said to him,—

'I allowed myself to be won far too easily,' and almost in the same breath she added,— 'but I could not help it, I love you dearer than my life; I loved you from the moment I saw you, and felt that fate had destined us for each other.'

Once he had doubted if she could love passionately, but he doubted no longer now. Behind that pure, virginal front, beat a heart with a capacity for love such as is granted to few women; but it was a heart as pure as her eyes and face, such a heart as warmed the breast of a Juliet, an Imogene, or Cordelia.

CHAPTER XV.

A BOHEMIAN PARTY.

ABOUT three days after Helen's arrival, Ralph told her that he expected a few of his friends would spend the evening with them. He made this announcement as he stood putting the finishing touches to the picture which was to make his fame—Maria Theresa confiding herself to the protection of the 'Hungarian Knights.'

Her face flushed with pleasure at the simple prospect.

'Oh, how nice! tell me all about them, dear.'

'Well, there's not much to tell, really. They are agreeable fellows, although not overburdened with this world's goods; like

myself, they deal largely in hope, and trust
to the future to reward their patient merit.
There's Bite, a journalist, splendid articles
he writes too ; then there's Sparkle the
comedy writer, he'll convulse you in five
minutes : he, by the way, is doing well since
that last hit of his.   There's my dear old
uncle, David Fairfax, artist like myself; I
shall be surprised if you don't fall in love
with him on the spot.   Young Gough, the
dramatic critic ; he's rather young at the
business yet, so he only reviews the small
theatres ; and his sister, an actress.'

'An actress!' cried Helen, joyfully.   It
will be remembered that she had once turned
her ambition stage-wards.   'Oh, how delightful! I am sure I shall make great friends
with her.'

'She isn't a swell, you know ; she only
does the gentlewoman and waiting-woman
kind of business,' said Ralph, carelessly.

Poor Helen's face fell at this announcement.   She had hoped to meet a stately
gifted being, who melted the house in Juliet,
and thrilled them in Lady Macbeth.   'I
daresay she will be very interesting to know,'

she said, in a more sobered manner; then she
added more timidly—' Ralph, dear, do you
know any great people,—people, I mean,
at the top of their professions, like Mr.
R——, the great painter, and Mrs. T——,
the novelist ? '

Ralph smiled. ' No, pet, not at present.
Mr. Scumble, who gets two thousand for a
portrait, and Mrs. Thrillum, who gets about
the same for a romance, would hardly condescend to partake of my hospitality. Great
people know you when you are great yourself.'

' I wish you were great,' said Helen, with
an unconscious sigh.

' I am trying to become so as hard as
I can, darling.'

She did not answer, but leaned back in
her chair, with the air of one in a profound
reverie. Ralph worked on steadily at his
picture ; presently he asked,—

' What are you thinking of, lady mine ? '

A faint flush stole over her cheek as she
met her lover's honest gaze. ' I was wondering if we should ever be rich.'

He answered lightly and cheerfully. ' I

think there are things less likely. I believe I shall succeed in my art, and in the present day, success means money. The public is a generous master, and pays merit not only in praise but specie.' He stole a look at her, and seeing that this hopeful prophecy had made her seem bright and sanguine, continued,—'Look at Wiggles; five years ago, he was nobody—did not get so much for his pictures as I do, and *now*—he gets eight hundred for a portrait, and has commissions for four years. Look at Splash again, a man with no pretensions to high art, his last picture—"Say good-bye to Grandmamma!"—sold for three thousand. The "Kiss and be Friends" of the same distinguished gentleman fetched three thousand five hundred.'

'Why don't you paint, "Say good-bye to Grandpapa!" Ralph?'

'It would be a copy, my dear; and besides my talent does not lie in the simple domestic. Splash is not an artist I should care to imitate; in fact, he has very few pretensions to art at all.'

'High art is a fine thing, no doubt;'

replied Helen, with the gentle obstinacy of womankind; 'but, all the same, I cannot help envying Mr. Splash's practical success.'

Silence succeeded ; Ralph did not care to dispute the justice of this last remark. How was it possible that Helen, who could know nothing of the principles of art, should comprehend his lofty scorn for the school of painting of which Mr Splash and his followers were the exponents ? This time it was she who first broke the silence.

'You know, Ralph dear, I think there is no disputing a few facts like these. It is nicer to ride than walk, to be waited upon than to wait upon one's self, to have handsome furniture, fine dresses, money to give away in charity, to possess educated acquaintances, than to be placed in a sphere where you can hope for none of these.'

Ralph laid down his brush, and came close to her. 'My darling,' he said tenderly, 'I am afraid you hanker after these things a little too much for your own peace.'

She smiled faintly. 'It is the first time I ever breathed such a wish to you.'

'Not a direct wish, perhaps, dear, but you

have many times let fall words that showed me very plainly your desires.'

'Is it a crime to wish to be rich, Ralph?'

'No, not a crime,' he answered quickly; then he added, in a nettled tone, and urged by the restless jealousy which ever accompanies ardent love,—'Would it not have been wiser to wait for a rich man who could have given you all these things, than link your fate with a poor, struggling artist, whose greatest treasure consists of hope?'

Her eyes filled with tears. 'You are unjust,' she said, in a low voice. 'I may be sordid in wishing for wealth, but I only wish that it should come through you.'

He caught her hand and covered it with kisses. 'Forgive me, my own darling, for being so hasty. It is but natural a girl so beautiful, so fitted to adorn the highest society, should pine for a different world. Have a little patience, and your ambition shall be gratified. A few years more of toil on my part, and all will come that you sigh for—furniture, horses, dresses, jewels, etc., etc.'

He ended with a little banter, and she smiled too, so these young people were reconciled, and went straight from this little discussion into love-making. But Ralph could not forget this incident. It saddened more than angered him, to think that she should desire anything in addition to his deep love. He forgot that he had his art to fall back upon, while she had no resource. 'This is her mother's evil teaching,' he said bitterly to himself. 'If my sweet girl is a little lower than the angels, it is the fault of that sordid woman.'

The first arrival among the guests of the evening was David Fairfax, a fine stalwart man of sixty, with a loud ringing voice and a hearty manner. His artistic eye dwelt with evident pleasure upon Helen's rare beauty, and he complimented her in his straightforward fashion.

'My dear young lady, I am delighted to find my nephew has made a choice which reflects so much credit on his taste and judgment. I am a judge of character, and I can see at a glance that you are as good as beautiful. There now, what an old savage

I am, for ladies' love unfit; I have made you blush.'

' I am very grateful for your good opinion,' said Helen, prettily.

David Fairfax laughed genially as was his wont, and turning to Mr. Vanstone, who stood near, smiling in a feeble way, said, 'If that sweet young lady were my daughter, sir, I should bear no good will to the fellow who came to steal her from me.'

To this sally, Gabriel Vanstone, not being a ready man, replied nothing; and David, seeing that there was not much to be extracted from the father, turned again to Helen.

' My dear, I believe my nephew Ralph is a sterling, upright, fine-hearted fellow, and deserves a good wife; but if, when you are married, you find anything to complain of, come to me, and I will thrash him into good behaviour myself.' And in spite of his years, he looked as if he could do it too. They all laughed at this invitation, of course, and Helen thought that if this genial old gentleman was a specimen of a Bohemian, the world of Bohemia must be a pleasant one to dwell in.

The next arrival was Mr. Bite, a man of a singularly placid and even benevolent cast of countenance, but, according to old Fairfax, who acted as master of the ceremonies to Helen, a terrible fellow.

'When Bite gets a pen in his hand, he's no longer a human being, but a pitiless demon. Take care not to offend him, Miss Vanstone, or he will flay you like a second Marsyas; but you don't know who Marsyas was, of course, how should you? You see I am so little accustomed to ladies' society, that I don't know how to talk to them. To return to our friend Bite,—it is reported that he is driving Lord Muddlebrain, the foreign secretary, to madness. I am quite certain that if the Fates were suddenly to exercise their shears on Bite, Lord Muddlebrain would dance a *bolero* in spite of his gout.'

All this was said in the presence and hearing of the gentleman described. To Helen's great astonishment, Mr. Bite listened with the utmost placidity to his old friend's banter, and only remarked quietly, when he had finished,—'Always a boy, David, always a boy!'

'That is why I wear so well, old friend, why I am hearty, and rosy, and stout, no lean-looking conspirator,' replied the whimsical artist. 'I have kept my sanguine temperament as my most precious possession; therefore do the world's troubles roll off my spirit, and therefore do I say with gentle Will, 'My age is as a lusty winter, frosty but kindly.'

There was a pause. 'Sparkle is late,' said Ralph Weldon.

'But he is coming, for I met him to-day in the Strand, and he told me so,' answered his uncle; then turning to Helen, he added, —'Have you ever met Sparkle?'

'No.'

'Ah! then I think you will be delighted with him. When he opens his mouth to speak, other persons are forced to open theirs to laugh. Nature gave Sparkle a face that would become a mute or an undertaker. As soon as he saw his reflection in the glass, he came to the conclusion that he had been badly treated, and resolved to cultivate a comic vein strangely at variance with his appearance. He succeeded; and you have the delightful incongruity of hearing the drollest things issuing from the most solemn-looking creature in the world.'

Hardly was the description finished, when Mr. Sparkle was announced, and certainly he looked solemn enough with a vengeance. He was also so very ugly, that Helen did not care to look at him too much. It seemed to her that there had been a steady depreciation in personal appearance since the advent of David. He was gentlemanly enough; but with regard to Mr. Bite, there was only one epithet which described him to Helen's satisfaction, and that was 'queer,'—a word by no means classic, but full of a subtle meaning to those who understand the mysteries of language. As to Mr. Sparkle,—his solemn and ugly countenance, his small body crowned by an enormous head, his short legs and long arms, presented a *tout ensemble* for which she could find no adjective in her vocabulary, save perhaps 'unnatural.'

To the young and ardent, appearances are much, if not everything, and a little chill crept over her at the thought that gentlemen of this kind were to be her life-long acquaintance. She waited eagerly for the door to open, in the hope of seeing somebody whom she would not be ashamed to be seen with in the 'Row' or at the 'Horticultural.' Fancy being escorted to a flower-show by Mr. Sparkle! The door opened at last, and Mr. Jones was announced, whom she had heard Ralph speak of as a rising young artist. He was rising six feet three in his stockings certainly, if that had anything to do with the matter; for the rest, he had a head of long, reddish hair, and a very plain face. Altogether, he was a hideous young man, and ran Mr. Sparkle hard for the first place in want of personal comeliness. Another very patent fact was, that although Mr. Jones might possess a fine sense of beauty in artistic matters, he had evidently none in the question of attire. His clothes were ill-made, his tie loosely arranged, and showing above his collar at the back.

This last arrival completely overwhelmed poor Helen. She could not understand what she saw. Surely, the world of Bohemia must contain some gentlemen of a more presentable appearance. She had seen the portrait of Mr. R——, the great painter, a handsome, aristocratic-looking man ; and young Catullus Brown, the promising poet, was a perfect Apollo. Could it be possible that Nature was in league with ill-fortune to set an opprobious mark upon those who did not succeed greatly in the world. She had not enough experience to know that there are extraordinary-looking creatures in every society, and that the reason they look less peculiar in the highest society than in any other, is because the elegance of the surroundings throws a veil over them. Here she was on the alert to discover faults ; at Lady Grahame's she would have entered the house with her mind fully made up that she was going to meet none but a superior class of beings. Like many others, she took the unknown for the magnificent, and *vice versa.*

The next arrival was a young actor, who proved to be a handsome, shapely fellow ; and after him came the actress and her brother. The brother was a little peculiar in appearance, but gentlemanly withal ; and the sister, plain of feature, but graceful and lady-like. Helen brightened up a bit at these last arrivals. Decidedly, the world of Bohemia was improving. It would, at least, have been ungrateful to entertain a bad opinion of them, since they all testified in the most unmistakeable manner that they admired her immensely. Even Mr. Sparkle, whose acquaintance lay chiefly among burlesque actresses, *et hoc genus omne*, and whose manners with ladies had in consequence acquired a somewhat free-and-easy tinge, treated her with the most respectful deference. In time, won by his evident desire to please, she forgot even his peculiar appearance and plain aspect.

In Bohemia there is no frigidity; in a very few moments the room was filled with the sound of everybody talking, and the conversation came borne to Helen's ears something after this fashion.

Mr. Sparkle, giving an account of his last piece to Clara Weldon.—'So I said to Quip, this is not the kind of fun that takes at all. You must bring in a comic cabman, or a footman, who drops his "h's," or something of that kind.'

Mr. Bite, discussing Politics with David Fairfax. — 'The policy of the present Government is characterised by feebleness, splutter, and an absolute disregard of the tax-payer. I have it on the highest authority that when it was proposed to give Lord Muddlebrain a seat in the Cabinet ten years ago, Lord P—— declared that he would not sit in the same room with such a noodle.'

Mr. Jones, discussing Art with Ralph Weldon.—'Stipple has ideas, some of them grand ones ; but what is the use of ideas to a man who cannot draw ? Good ideas coupled with bad drawing are most offensive.'

Ralph Weldon, who has a higher opinion of Mr. Stipple than his friend.—'Not so offensive as good drawing without an idea, old fellow, like Splash's rubbish, eh ?'

The Actor, detailing the gossip of the green room to the actress's brother.—'There's no doubt in the matter ; she was actually intoxicated when she came on the stage, and had the greatest difficulty to keep herself from falling. E—— told me he never felt so disgusted in his life as at having to go through the piece with her. You've heard about young Barry, of course? No!—well, the other night he was playing at Mrs. F——'s theatre, and in the piece she considered he took hold of her too roughly. By-gad, sir, when the curtain was down, she slapped his face before them all. Barry swears he'll bring an action.'

While all this chatter went on, Helen was having a long conversation about the stage with the actress, to whom she confided, somewhat bashfully, that she had herself once contemplated `entering the theatrical profession.

The young lady smiled pityingly.

' Ah ! my dear Miss Vanstone, I am glad, for your own sake, you did not. Family misfortunes compelled me to turn actress, but it is one of the hardest modes of getting a livelihood. When I first took to it, I thought, as no doubt you have done, that it would be a fine thing to play " Juliet " and the " Lady of Lyons " before applauding audiences ; but that is the most rosy side of the picture. I have never played Juliet yet, and I don't suppose I ever shall.'

She examined Helen critically for a few seconds, and then added,—

'But you might have had a very good chance of succeeding on the stage, for, of course, your appearance is so greatly in your favour.'

Helen blushed at the compliment, and her friend, noting this feminine weakness, asked with a smile,—

'Do you think you could have made yourself brazen enough for our profession?'

'I am afraid, when it came to the pinch, I could never have faced the footlights.'

Taking advantage of a temporary lull in the Babel, David Fairfax stood up, and called out in his hearty tones,—

'Ladies and Gentlemen, I am going to ask our friend Sparkle to give us a little entertainment of his own arranging.'

Hereupon Mr. Sparkle put his hand upon his heart, and bowing profoundly, answered in a voice of assumed bashfulness,—

'Really, unaccustomed as I am to public speaking—'

Whereupon there was a loud laugh from

all who understood the gentleman's peculiar humour.

These preliminaries having been settled, Mr. Sparkle gave them an imitation of amateur performers at Penny Readings, and in five minutes the audience was fairly convulsed, Helen among the number. There was the bleating vicar, who read the 'May Queen' in much the same tone as he would read the Psalms ; the young man with a cold in his head, who *would* recite ' The Raven ;' and a lot of other imitations remarkable for their mirth-moving powers. Helen had never seen anything of this kind before, and she was delighted with it all.

The ball having once been set in motion, it was constantly kept going by the others. The actor and actress did the cottage scene from the ' Lady of Lyons,' which made Helen weep copiously. Bite, the critical, the ferocious, sang a comic song. Mr. Jones played a sonata, which was not so entertaining, as there were few in the room who cared much about music. Ralph recited the ' Ride to Ghent,' and splendidly he did it, in the judgment of one young person, at all events.

Then, when everybody had done his best in turn, they came back again to Sparkle, who gave them an imitation of a popular lady singer noted, for her love of runs and flourishes. Sparkle, the actor and actress, were the lions of the evening ; the efforts of the others fell flat after theirs, like soda-water after champagne.

The evening flew on wings, and Helen felt sorry when supper was announced, for it meant an end of those friendly performances. Still, it was by no means a dull meal ; the table was kept in a roar, chiefly with the drollery of Sparkle. Then they finished the evening with proposing healths ; and, after a few had been drank, Mr. Sparkle rose, and begged leave to propose the toast of the evening. Everybody was silent, and Helen, who had a presentiment of what was coming, blushed violently. The speech was as follows, delivered in a serious and earnest voice,—

' Ladies and Gentlemen,—We have already testified our good feelings towards our host, and, speaking for all of us, I may emphatically say, it was no mere empty form of compliment. Ralph Weldon is our friend, our very dear friend, of many years' standing. Side by side, shoulder to shoulder, we have marched on together like hardy soldiers, sometimes with very little in our knapsacks, fighting the hard and stern battle of life. Ladies and Gentlemen, we can look back without regret, and we can also look forward with hope. His future is gilded with hope of the most radiant description. If Ralph Weldon is dear to us as an old Bohemian comrade and brother, the lady who is about to become his wife must be dear to us too. I beg to propose long life, health, and happiness to Miss Vanstone, the future wife of Ralph Weldon, whose beauty and grace justly earn for her the title of Queen of Bohemia !'

Mr. Sparkle ceased amid a whirlwind of applause, and the health of the ' Queen of Bohemia !' was drunk with the greatest enthusiasm. Gladly would she have spoken a few grateful words in reply, but utterance and power to arrange her ideas both failed her, and Ralph returned thanks on her behalf. Five minutes afterwards there was a general rush to catch the last train to town, and the cottage returned to its normal quietude.

'Have you enjoyed yourself, darling?' asked Ralph, when they were alone.

'Oh, so much. I think Bohemia is a delightful world, and the dwellers therein the most delightful people.'

He kissed her gladly, with a happy look on his face. But in spite of her sincere assurance, there never was a girl who had less in common with Bohemianism than Helen Vanstone. First views of all things are notoriously deceptive, and at present her tastes and aspirations pointed towards a very different sphere.

Something of all this flashed through his own mind, but he consoled himself with the recollection of how dearly she loved him, and felt sure that for his sake she would love his world.

CHAPTER XVI.

YOUTHFUL HEARTS.

'WHAT are you thinking about, Helen?' cried Ralph.

It was the day after the Bohemian party. The young people were seated on the lawn, basking in the sun, Helen holding a dainty parasol to shield her face from the rays, her lover smoking a cigarette, and feasting his eyes upon her delicate beauty. At first she had felt rather bashful under his constant scrutiny; but when he told her, with the greatest gravity, that it was impossible for a true lover to keep his gaze away from his mistress, she nerved herself to stand the ordeal, and was surprised to find that a couple of days' practice had rendered her

perfectly hardened. There had been silence
between them for some time, and Helen
had fallen into a reverie, hence his question.

'Perhaps if I tell you, I shall make you
vain,' she replied.

'Let me beg of you to run the risk, my
darling.'

'Well, then, Ralph, I was wondering if
our life could always be as happy as it is
now ; because, you know, most people of
experience tell you that married men soon
grow cross and irritable.'

Ralph muttered to himself, 'That's an
arrow out of my sweet friend, Mrs. Vanstone's quiver.' Then he said aloud, 'And
by a natural application, you began to ask
yourself whether Ralph Weldon would grow
cross and irritable with his beloved Helen ?'

'Just so ; and I came to the conclusion
that I had not much to dread. I don't set
up for a great judge of character, Ralph, my
experience of your sex being dreadfully
limited ; but with women, instinct often
supplies the place of experience.' She
paused a moment, and then, placing one
hand in his, and looking into his face with

an expression of the most perfect love, added, 'My instinct tells me that you are not like ordinary men, selfish, fickle, unreasonable. I believe that twenty years hence I shall be as dear to you as I am now, in the bloom of our youth and romance.'

He carried her hand to his lips. 'Dearer, my sweet love, if it be possible to love more than I do now!'

'How strange that I, of all girls, should have fallen in love,' she was beginning, with innocent gravity, when he interrupted her.

'Say rather, how strange that you should not have done so. It would be an outrage to imagine such beauty as yours without the Promethian spark that makes it divine. It would have been as anomalous as a scentless rose or a songless nightingale.'

'You will make me most preposterously vain, sir,' she answered, assuming a severe look. 'But really, Ralph, I always thought I must be a very cold creature. I never remember to have looked on any of your sex with approbation, or to have had the least desire for those innocent flirtations in which other girls take delight. I had long

made up my mind I should never love anybody but mamma.'

'You were waiting for the right man,
you discerning young lady. Now, Helen, I
want you to candidly answer me one question—"What opinion did you form of me on
the first night of our acquaintance, when I
came to see your father on business, you
know ?"'

'Let me think a little, Mr. Inquisitive.
Well, in the first place, I certainly thought
you a superior being to the few men I had
come into contact with before ; and then, am I
not dreadfully forward in confessing all this ?
I remember that I went to bed earlier than
usual, to have a little extra think about you.'

'You sweet angel! Helen, that was love
at first sight.'

'Perhaps not. Let us see if we cannot
find another reason,' she answered, playfully.
'I led a very lonely life, visitors were excessively rare ; my proceeding might have been
the same with any other tolerable-looking
young gentleman.'

'Oh, Helen! Helen! can you look me in
the face, and say that your heart did not tell

you there was a mysterious affinity between our souls?'

'What! after ten minutes' interview? You dear old goose! Now, come, I have satisfied your curiosity; it is your turn. What did you think of me?'

She was looking at him with one of her most charming expressions; her eyes were sparkling with happiness, with that kind of joy which comes only in youth, and springs from only one source—gratified affection. Her lips were parted in a smile that made her look like a young Hebe. As Ralph Weldon gazed on her thus, he felt almost mad with delight to think that this radiant creature would one day be his own. A flush of deep feeling burned on his cheek as he answered,—

'I thought you were such a woman as I might have pictured in my dreams, but could have never hoped to meet out of dreamland. Your gestures, your voice, your grace dwelt on my memory, leaving there an imperishable record. I carried your presence with me from your home; I shut my eyes, but still you stood before me, graceful, gracious,

and beautiful as I had just beheld you. I
saw you again in my sleep, and when I awoke,
I knew for certain that I had found my
ideal,—the woman who would make of the
man who loved her an artist or a poet. I
began to realise the matchless conceptions of
the great creators,—Juliet, Marguerite, Imogene,—and you seemed to me one worthy,
like them, of the most exalted passion.'

The tears gathered in her eyes as he
spoke thus, his tones even more than his
words bearing witness to his fervent love;
then, half ashamed of her emotion, she said
in a sprightly tone, 'I ought to inspire you
with the subject for a grand picture.'

What he would have replied to this must
be left to conjecture, for Mr. Vanstone came
sauntering towards them with a cigar in his
mouth. Ralph would have preferred that he
should not have made his appearance at that
exact moment; but, under the circumstances,
he was a necessary encumbrance, and to
treat him with courtesy was a duty. One
thing must be said in his praise: he was
much more considerate to the young people
than his wife would have been; but then he

had known the meaning of love, while she never had.

'A charming little place this, Weldon, my boy. It makes me shudder to think of Thomas Street after it,' remarked the old gentleman, as he carefully deposited himself on the grass.

'Why don't you take a house in the country? As you have no occupation, it doesn't matter where you live,' said Ralph.

'Humph! it's inconvenient to get to the club,' answered Mr. Vanstone. A few moments' reflection had convinced him that permanent residence in the country would mean staying at home on wet and unpropitious nights, in the company of a snappish spouse. Ralph saw what was passing in his mind, and said, with some slyness,—

'But I forget, you are not a domesticated character.'

The poor old gentleman just smiled, and then sighed.

'No, I have no encouragement to be so,' he said, in an accent that conveyed volumes.

Helen leaned forward and shook her finger playfully at him,—

'Papa, that is an insinuation. If you had ever been a domesticated character, you would not have behaved so badly in your youth. Look at the state I am reduced to through your wickedness.'

'Ah yes, child, I daresay I deserve all I've got,' assented the old gentleman, with a melancholy smile.

'O come, don't let us be mournful,' she cried, in a cheerful tone, and putting her arms round his neck, she gave him a hearty kiss. 'There, you are not a bad old papa after all, although I ought to have been an heiress instead of a poor beggar, with about five shillings pocket-money, and a sovereign to put in my purse on grand occasions, although, like the "Vicar of Wakefield's" daughter, I have strict injunctions not to change it.'

'You shall have a banking account all to yourself one day,' said Ralph, in a sanguine tone. 'It would be worth a hundred pounds to see you write your first cheque.'

'My dear Ralph! I should be writing cheques all day for the first month, till the novelty wore off.'

'That reminds me of a story I once read,'

interposed Mr. Vanstone. 'A certain king of O-why-hee had built for him a house after the most approved modern pattern. The thing about it that most astonished the savage monarch was the staircase; and he was so delighted with this novel feature in architecture, that he amused himself by running up and down it all day!'

'And what about the ponies I promised you? would you be driving them about all day for the first month?' asked Ralph.

In discussing that fairy future when he was to get two thousand pounds for a picture, it had been arranged between these young people that a pair of ponies for Helen's special use would be an indispensable luxury, quite apart from the more imposing carriage which was to convey them to dinners and parties.

It was in painting such fancy pictures that they passed the time. Lovers who are not overburdened with this world's goods must perforce live largely on hope, and I am not sure that in many cases it is not an invigorating food. The beauty of the artistic professions is that they give so wide a field for the exercise of the imaginative faculty, and

tone down the stern realities of life. A poor
solicitor or a poor parson must of necessity
be bounded in his views; many other favouring circumstances besides ability being necessary to bring the one an immense practice or
make the other a bishop. But to the artist,
the poet, the musician, the morrow may
bring fame and wealth, although he be in
poverty to-day: one splendid picture, one
exquisite poem, one grand opera, may in a
few hours lift him from destitution to affluence. Suppose Ralph Weldon had been a
clerk, could Helen have ever looked forward
to the advent of those ponies with any
degree of confidence? It is true that in-
dustrious clerks are sometimes taken into
partnership, but how rarely, and under what
exceptional circumstances. But now, so long
as Ralph could wield a brush, so long as
there remained a public to appeal to, fortune
was not impossible—was only delayed in its
arrival. If 'Maria Theresa' did not make
his fame, why, his next great picture might
do so! and if, for some almost unaccountable
reason or another, that failed, the one after
would be more successful; and so on *ad infi-*

nitum.   On the whole, she congratulated herself on the fact that she was going to marry a man belonging to a profession in which hope played so large a part.

Fortunately for the continuous indulgence of her roseate dreams, Helen had that strong faith in her lover which made her believe that success was only a question of time, and that the public must ultimately discover the merit which was already patent to her discerning vision.   In painting, too, it happened that without much technical knowledge, she had certain instincts which enabled her to tell a good picture after a few glances, and Ralph found himself hugely comforted by her sanguine prophecies.   He had that belief in his own powers without which hardly any man can achieve greatness ; but 'hope deferred maketh the heart sick,' and he had so often anticipated a triumph, which had never come, that sometimes he grew despondent.

'Do you *really* think this is a *great* picture ?' he used to say to her often, as they were together in his studio.   'Or is it going to turn out an ambitious failure ?'

Then she always replied firmly she was sure it would make his reputation ; and she said this from conviction, not merely from a desire to keep up his spirits. And after this encouragement, he always worked with greater gusto than before.

To a man fighting the battle of life, it is an inestimable blessing to meet a woman who thoroughly believes in him. Her inspiring words of praise act as a greater spur than the moderate approval of colder critics. For, although she may have less knowledge than they, her love gives her a greater insight into the capacity of her lover ; she alone knows his hidden thoughts, his clearest ambitions, his strength and weakness ; she alone sees him in his loftiest as well as his lowest moments, for to her he displays the enthusiasm he would be ashamed to exhibit to the world.

It was perhaps a perception of this truth that made Ralph say to her, ' I believe there is no inspiration more divine than that which is given by love. I have a new incentive now to prove myself worthy of your good opinion.'

CHAPTER XVII.

RALPH'S HISTORY.

'HELEN, you remember my telling you that there had been certain things in my past history which had cast a deep shadow over my life?' he asked her one evening, as they went gliding down the river in his boat. They were alone that evening, for Clara Weldon had stayed at home with a bad headache.

'I remember it perfectly, and you promised that you would keep no secrets from me,' answered the girl, gravely.

He ceased rowing, and let the ‘boat float on with the current.

'The story I am going to tell you, dearest, is a very sad one. I have an uneasy conviction that I ought to have told it long ago, if not to you, at least to your parents.'

She looked at him in amazement, and her colour faded slightly, for his manner was so grave and solemn, that it seemed to her significant of some evil that might imperil their love. He understood that look of surprise mingled with dread, and answered it immediately.

'With some women the knowledge that I am going to impart to you might have influenced their decision. But I fancy I have read your character well enough to be sure that when you have heard this story, you will pity rather than blame my weakness. When I stood beside you that night on which we gathered the roses, and saw your sweet eyes shining up to mine with such love and trust in their clear depths, I was a coward, Helen. I could not then have uttered a word which might have led you to suppose that there was or might be even the shadow of a barrier between our hearts.'

She was quite pale now, and her heart was throbbing painfully with the dread of this revelation which was prefaced so gravely.

Was the life of sunshine and perfume in which she had been revelling for the last few weeks, only, after all, a cheating dream, from which she was to be suddenly and rudely awakened by the touch of some ghostly and hidden skeleton, who came creeping out of the shadows of the past? In her horror she did not know what to think, what shape to give to the evil that was impending. This man might have committed some sin past redemption, even some crime that would drag after it the Nemesis of the law.

As he noted the agonised expression on her face, it struck him, for the first time, that the solemnity of his manner might have given birth to such apprehensions as these.

'There is no need for alarm, my darling,' he said tenderly. 'The barrier between us, if such should exist, was built not by me, but by the hands of others; and the heart of her who built it was innocent of every sin, save that which man's perfidy and lawlessness often converts into a sin,—the faculty of loving not wisely but too well.'

She gave a long sigh of relief as she

listened to those reassuring words. Thank
heaven, he at least was free! The errors
and faults of others, least of all the errors
and faults of a woman, as he indicated that
they were, could not lower *him*. Whatever
might be the details of this sad story to
which she was about to lend her ears, she
felt sure that their recital could not dim for
long the sunshine of their hearts.

And then, amid the fading light and the
falling shadows, he told her the history of
his past.

'When I go back to the earliest days
of my childhood, there comes to me the
recollection of a little house in the country,
something like my own now, with a pretty,
spacious garden, in which I and Clara used
to play about, while my mother sat watching
us from under the shade of a grand old tree
that flourished at the bottom of the lawn.

'I can recall my mother's face perfectly
in those days, the days of her youth, for she
was not more than twenty-seven then. She
was a beautiful woman, with large dark eyes,
and glossy dark hair like your own, only I
never saw on her features the sunlight that

falls upon yours, for the summer had gone out of her life years ago, and her smiles issued from a broken heart.

'Both Clara and I, as soon as we were able to reason and think a little, noticed this constant sadness, which would end often in tears as we all sat together,—and puzzled our small minds in endeavours to discover the cause. Our life was a dull one; no visitors save one, who, we were told, was our uncle, ever relieved the monotony. Often and often did we put to her questions concerning our relatives, and the father whom we imagined to be dead; and, young as we were, we discovered in her answers a certain air of embarrassment and mystery that puzzled us still more.

'The years glided by, and with an instinctive feeling that these questions gave pain to our mother, we had long discontinued them. It was not until I had reached fifteen that we were made acquainted with the secret of our birth, and perhaps but for stern necessity we should never have known it to the day of her death.

'I entered her room casually one afternoon, and found her seated in an attitude of the deepest dejection, her face bathed in tears, and an open letter which had dropped from her hands to the floor. At the sight of me she raised her head, and, opening her arms, folded me to her breast. I can feel her tears dropping on my cheek now, and hear again the mournful tones in which she kept repeating the words, " My poor, poor Ralph ! my poor, unhappy boy."

' And, then slowly, for the words fell from her as if they had been drops of blood wrung from her heart, she told me the sad story of her wrongs and suffering.

' Sixteen years ago, in the town of her birth, she made the acquaintance of a young officer. She was the daughter of a not very flourishing surgeon. He was a man of birth and high connexion, the heir to large estates. Their is no need to sketch the history of their attachment, of their clandestine meetings, of the world-worn excuses he put forth for not wooing her in an open manner, —the dread of disinheritance through a father's anger, the loss of great expectations from other quarters, and all the other methods by which a man succeeds in masking his villany from the eyes of the woman who loves him. He persuaded her to come up to London in order to be married privately to him.

'They were married, as she thought. Not until he grew tired of her did she learn the truth, that it was a sham, that the priest who read over the service was a creature of his own. I pass by any description of her agony when she discovered this treachery; and its poignancy was increased by knowing that she could blame none but herself and her seducer. He tired of her sooner than the ordinary run of villains, and six months after Clara was born, he left her with a coldly-worded letter, in which he informed her that, as he was soon going to be married to a girl belonging to his own rank of life, it was better that they should separate.

' Perhaps the discovery of his utter heartlessness helped to cure my mother of her love for the worthless scoundrel; at any rate, she acted like a woman of courage and spirit, threatening him that if he did not make a decent provision for herself and her unhappy children, she would expose him to the woman he was going to marry. This threat brought him to terms, for his future wife was both an heiress and a woman of high tone and principle. As long as that wife lived, he carried out his covenant faithfully ; but three months after her death, he sent the letter which I had seen on the floor, and which my mother read to me. It was headed, " Dear Mrs. Weldon," and contained a business-like and formal announcement to the effect that, in view of his increasing expenses, he would find it quite impossible to pay for the future so large a sum as he had hitherto done, and must reduce it to a hundred a-year.

'After she had recovered from the first shock of this cruel intelligence, my mother sent for our uncle, a kindly, genial bachelor, who followed the profession of an artist with but scant success, and asked his advice. We were practically thrown upon the world ; our education was stopped, and our outlook was of the gloomiest. The paltry sum would just suffice to give us shelter and food enough to keep us from starving.

'We were brought to a dead-lock. Both I and my sister had early manifested a love for art, and had received instruction from my uncle. It was possible that in time we might be able to get our living as artists, but this was, of course, problematical, and the present pressed heavily upon us. Money must be got somehow at once, and the question was, how could this be done? It seemed that there was nothing left for me but that refuge of the destitute—a clerkship. My poor mother, who was ambitious for her children, wept copiously at the gloomy prospect of her darling son having to pass his days on a four-legged stool in some dingy office.

'My uncle, one of the best-hearted men in the world, was moved by her grief. "I wish to Heaven I could devise some better plans for him, my dear," he said kindly; "but what can the poor lad do without means? I live from hand to mouth myself, as you know, and could not scrape together a hundred pounds to help him. And it would take ten times that sum to start him in anything respectable, even if he had business knowledge."

'"I know that too well," sobbed my poor,

dejected mother. Suddenly a bright idea came into my uncle's head. " Listen to me, Mabel. I have a notion that you might do something with this villain by a personal interview. When you have got a man face to face, you can deal better with him than by letters."

' My mother gave a shiver at the prospect. " I think I would sooner die than meet that man again, David ; and you do not know his nature, made up as it is of cruelty and light- ness. I should make no impression on him."

' " I am not so sure of that," replied her brother, shaking his head. " The scoundrel cared for you once, and the sight of your suffering might soften his heart. Take your boy with you ; he is a fine young fellow, of whom a father ought to be proud. The interview must prove a painful one, I am aware ; but, for the sake of your children, it is necessary that you should leave no stone unturned."

' At those words, my mother glanced from me to Clara, and back again from Clara to me, with eyes that overflowed with tears.

' " For the sake of my children, I will con- quer my own repugnance," she said, in a brave voice. "You inspire me with faith, David; it is impossible that he can look on this dear boy without some natural emotions. His letter is dated from his country place. I will take Ralph down with me to-morrow, and we will enter together the home that by right belongs to me and these darlings."

'I can see her now as she uttered that brave resolve, a crimson flush lighting up the pale, wan cheek, and a stedfast light gathering into those beautiful dark eyes, which are so like your own.

'"Yes," she resumed, in a softer tone, "when his glance falls upon this boy, his heir and first-born in the sight of heaven, if not of man, and I tell him of the proud hopes and dreams that I have indulged in when I pictured his future, he may return to a sense of what he owes to me and to my helpless children."

'She placed one hand on my head, and drew me to her breast with the other.

'"Ralph, my darling boy," she whispered to me, "we will go to your father to-morrow."'

END OF VOL. I.